HOT SINATRA

A novel by
Axel Howerton

FIRST EDITION SOFTCOVER
ISBN: 1622535014
ISBN-13: 978-1-62253-501-9

Edited by William Hampton and Lane Diamond

Printed in the U.S.A.

www.EvolvedPub.com
Evolved Publishing LLC
Cartersville, Georgia

Hot Sinatra is a work of fiction. All names, characters, places, and incidents are the product of the author's imagination, or are used fictitiously. Any resemblance to actual events or persons, living or dead, is entirely coincidental.

Printed in Book Antiqua font.

DEDICATION:

For Foxy & Francis, and my dear ol' Grandad,
Gone, but never forgotten.

Chapter 1

I pulled up to the sprawling collection of Spanish villa-style buildings affectionately referred to as the "Flo-Ho Arms," just as a slow-moving posse of old men shambled out onto the front lawn like plaid-suited zombies—all giant sunglasses and gleaming metal walkers. I crept up the shallow front steps, and they waved, hollering their greetings as they'd long been taught—the civilized way to behave.

Pops had been like that. Always said hello to people he'd never met before, wished them well, told them to have a good day. He'd always meant it too. You never saw that in people under sixty anymore. Nobody just said 'Hi' to strangers on the street anymore. General consensus in many parts of L.A. was that you'd just as likely get a knife to the face as a smile or a handshake.

So I took a second and offered a lazy wave back and shouted, "Looks like a nice warm day shaping up there." A terrible cliché, but what the hell else did they have to talk about?

Most of them had been abandoned here like old furniture. At best, they got visits on the weekend from bored grandkids that they'd never met on the outside. They'd get sad, pitying glances from their condescending middle-aged "kids," who'd act as if there was something these poor old bastards could have done to not end up in a place like this—more of a prison than most federal pens.

Pops had stayed in a place like this as he approached the end, but not because he needed to be. I figured part of him wanted to plant the seeds of dissent among his fellows, prove that they didn't have to burn out, or fade away. Even fighting cancer and a couple of strokes, Pops walked the walk all the way, while most of us just toddled along behind him.

I continued up the stone walkway and through the ornate glass doors into the place. The first thing you noticed, upon entering the Florence Henderson Continuing Care Center, was the expanse of the modern open foyer. Then the lingering stench of bleach and urine attacked.

Pops went out in a place like this, riddled with cancer and fighting to breathe, yet tough as nails to the end. The day before he passed away, he was still as charming as the devil himself, flirting with the young nurses and demanding steak dinner. He never would have come out on a call like this. He would have politely declined and offered some alternate agency that could be of more help.

I shook off the stench of death and incontinence and, after a few conflicting sets of directions from some stoned orderlies, made my way to room 224.

The first thing Obadiah Stetch noticed was my hat. "What are you supposed to be, Bogey or something? Ain't nobody wore them hats in years. You look fucking ridiculous. At least wear a suit with it. What kind of gumshoe are you, anyway? You're supposed to be Moe Rossi's boy, aren't you?"

"Grandson."

"Right. You don't really look like him, do you? He was a handsome fucker, pulled all kinds of pussy. He never would have worn a fucking hat like that. Stupid 'Rat Pack' fucking thing."

My 1953 Royal Stetson fedora had, in fact, been my grandfather's hat. Pop's hat. People assumed I wore the hats as a joke, to be ironic — some attention-craving hipster playing P.I. dress-up. I took a lot of shit about the hats. I certainly didn't need to hear it again from some ancient, mouthy jerk-off with something to prove from the confines of what would probably be his deathbed.

I took it off and settled myself in a chair near the bed, folding my denim-clad legs and setting the hat on my knee. So far, my hunch had been correct: Obadiah Stetch didn't rate the trouble of putting on a suit.

"Mr. Stetch, did you just call me down here to have someone to spit insults at? Or do we actually have some business to discuss?"

He picked thick-framed glasses from somewhere in the mess of sheets covering his legs, and searched my face through even thicker lenses that magnified his rheumy eyes and made him look like an old bulldog.

"No, kid, I got a job for you. If you can handle it, that is."

I took a second to brush off his stale and obnoxious breath, along with some imaginary dust on my leg.

"Well, that all depends on the job, doesn't it, Mr. Stetch?"

The old bastard took the glasses back off, apparently satisfied that I had moxie enough to be worth his time. Obie Stetch had been a rich, powerful and fairly notorious man-about-town in his day. That day had passed three decades ago. Stetch had been a club owner, musical agent, boxing promoter, and self-involved prick as far back as the forties. Now he was another old man facing a lazy death and a rapidly declining amount of respect from the world.

I figured throwing him a bone wouldn't kill me. "Mr. Stetch, sir, I know you're an important man who probably has other business to deal with today, so why don't we get down to why I'm here."

He took the bait as most lonely old pricks do, and straightened in his bed, a glimmer of life lifting a snarl onto his face. "Don't need to kiss my ass, kid. But you're all right. I think we can do business."

He hefted a book out of nowhere, one of those pleather-bound photo albums that are supposed to look like an impressive volume of English poetry, and laid it open on the sheets.

I was hoping he was at least looking for something pertinent to the conversation.

He rambled on as he flipped through the book. "This is bullshit, having to meet like this, in a goddamn hospital room. Once I'm fixed up, you come see me at the house. We'll have a drink by the pool, out in the sun. This is bullshit. Fucking doctors don't know a thing."

He stopped his flipping and stabbed a gnarled old finger at a photo of a younger version of himself, standing with a young Frank Sinatra in front of a stage full of musicians. Circa 1948, no doubt, on account of the banner hanging over the stage that said, "Happy New Year 1948."

"That's me with Sinatra in 1948. We were close personal friends. Frank once gave me the five thousand-dollar Rolex off his own wrist. He was a gentleman, knew how to treat important people like Obadiah Stetch!"

I rolled my eyes and held back the mounting urge to grab the book and smack him with it.

"He was playing my place in Van Nuys: The Mozambique. I had a very important, very rare piece of wax cut from that show. You know what a record is, kid?"

I bit down on the inside of my cheek and redoubled my efforts not to slap him on his bald spot.

"That record was made for me by my late wife, one of the greatest gifts I've ever received. I had it here with me. It was framed up on the wall there...."

He pointed absently at a spot on the wall where the paint was a shade darker in the rectangular shape of a picture frame. A dozen other pictures and framed memorabilia surrounded the bare spot, but it was clear by its position in the center that it was the *piece de resistance*.

"Somebody stole it?"

"Oh, somebody give that boy a lolli. Yeah, somebody stole it, you shit-for-brains! And I fucking want it back. Nobody steals from Obie Stetch. I run this goddamn town!"

I'd been regretting taking Stetch's call since I hung up the phone that morning, but at this point all I wanted was to get up and walk out and straight into the bar across the street. They'd have coffee, right? Just a coffee. Of course, if he kept up his deluded, self-serving tantrums, I'd probably be knee-deep in scotch five minutes after I left, and *that* I would most certainly regret.

I took a deep breath of decrepit ass chased with a blast of industrial antiseptic, and immediately regretted that as well. "Any idea who would have taken it?"

His puckered little bulldog face lit up scarlet. "Do you have any idea who you're talking to, you little shit? I was making gold fucking records before your mama was a bulge in your grandaddy's pants. Yeah, I got some ideas. Yeah, because *nobody* would steal an autographed fucking *Sinatra* record. You *fuck!*" Thick spittle foamed at the corners of his mouth, sputtering and spraying forth as if from an expired fire extinguisher

A fat nurse with too much blush stuck her face around the corner with a stern look of disapproval. I shrugged innocently for her, trying to convey the situation, of which she was probably well aware. If he acted like this now, he probably did it all the time. Ancient lunatics were probably part and parcel. Nothing to see here.

"Everything all right in here, Mr. Stetch? If you don't calm down we'll have to sedate you again."

"Fuck you!" His red face darkened a shade. "Who the fuck do you think you are? I could buy and fucking sell you in a heartbeat!"

She clucked her tongue and shook her head, then disappeared from the doorway.

I stood up and twisted my head to crack the tension out of my neck. I wanted to head-butt the old cocksucker. Instead, I leaned in close to his bed and gave him the goods in as harsh a whisper as I could manage without drawing attention from the nurses station outside.

"Listen, you belligerent old fart, you'd have to be stupid to put an autographed Sinatra record on the wall and *not* expect somebody to steal it. You want me to find it? Cut me some slack. Answer a few questions—without being a delusional prick—and maybe I can help you. Keep acting like a spoiled four-year-old, and I walk."

I stood there, trying to be menacing, while he composed himself, lay back, and drew a deep breath of resignation.

"All right, I'm sorry, kid. Maybe we should finish this some other time. You come up to my office on Monday. I got lunch with Michael Jackson's agent this afternoon. You know Michael Jackson? That kid is gonna hit it big, mark my words. Weird fucking blackie, but he's got some fucking pipes. I think he may be a cake-boy, you know what I mean? Likes it in the ass."

Jesus H. Addle-brained Christ, Obadiah Stetch was a piece of work. I couldn't even fathom what an unbelievable scumbag he must have been when he was out on the loose with money and power and youth to spare. I thought of trying to knock some sense into him, imagined myself wrapping the cord from one of his machines around his scrawny neck, maybe slapping him with that photo album until his spindly little hate-filled head popped off. Instead, I forced myself to focus on the work, like Pops always told me. *Everybody's an asshole. You have to be able to work around 'em.* Pops had never lost his mind, never turned into one of these cartoonish old farts with a walker yelling about kids on the lawn.

I tried to summon some sympathy for Stetch, but came up short. "Look, Stetch, you've got a lot of impressive trinkets up there—more than any sane person would keep out in a place like this, but I get it. You want everybody to know that you used to be a big shot. They took the one piece. Only that one. That speaks to pre-meditation and motive. That means that whoever took the Sinatra record was only after the Sinatra record. Was there anyone who showed an interest in it? Anyone who would have profited unusually from that one piece?"

"I've been calling some old friends. See if they know where I left it."

"Left it? Did you lose it? Or did it get stolen? Make up your goddamn mind, Stetch!"

"Hey! My kind of friends, they'll take some real interest in helping out. They'll put some feet on the street for you, get answers. I don't even know why I called you. You used to be the best. Look at you now. Moe Rossi. Big Man."

"Moe Rossi was my grandfather, you batshit old goon." I shook my head and sat back, frustrated. I'd give it one more shot and try to keep the disdain to a visible minimum.

"Mr. Stetch, I understand you're a very important and busy man, so if you could just give me the names of anyone you suspect might have taken the record...."

I hoped to Christ that he was paying attention and understood. If not, the whole morning was a waste of my time and his money, although I was much less worried about his pockets than my sleep schedule. He sat heavy, slumped forward. I was beginning to think he'd fallen asleep, or died while I was talking, when he suddenly sat bolt upright with a hard glint in his eye.

"Ramone?"

"Who is Ramone? One of the people here in the hospital?"

"Ramone." He repeated, flipping the photo book open again and stopping on the picture he'd shown me before. He jabbed his finger at a trumpet player in the background, a real *pachuco* with a pencil thin moustache and slick hair. He looked like a stereotypical Big Band musician—like DeNiro in New York, New York.

"It couldn't be Ramone. He's dead. Been dead thirty-some years. Maybe one of his people...."

How could I take anything he said at face value? He was constantly self-aggrandizing, or lost in time, or losing his mind, or just plain lying his ass off.

"So, Ramone... he died when, exactly?"

"I just said—'48, right after these pictures were taken."

"That would be more than sixty years ago, Stetch. I think we can cross him off the list of suspects."

"You think I don't know that? You fucking guido punk! Come in here and try to push me around, will you, Tony?" He hollered, waving his glasses around for effect.

I stared a hole through him, hoping it would bear fruit and settle him down a little. Whether it was my eyeballing him, or he just wore himself out, he shrunk back against the pillow. All the energy that had been pouring out of him moments before was gone, replaced by clear eyes and a set jaw. It would be a miracle if I could keep myself from ending up on the wrong end of a bottle after talking to that batshit codger.

"Are you finished?" I growled at him. "You were telling me who you thought might have stolen the record."

"Look, anybody could have stolen it. Fuckin' Viet-Cong nurses and spic janitors they have in this fucking place. Every one of 'em is a goddamn thief. Come to think of it, there's a kid works here, named Enrique, looks just like old Ramone. I never realized it until just now. I knew there was a reason I didn't like that fucking beaner kid, sniffing around my room all the time. Probably some grandkid or something."

I stood up and looked through the windows to see if there were any Hispanic kids working in the area. All I could see was the fat nurse and a couple of shady-looking white dudes in orderly jackets.

"I'll check out Enrique. Now why do you think this *Ramone* would have something to do with it?"

"That Mex hump tried to steal it from me back then. He played horns on the gig and was always trying to get his hands on the record to prove it. He was crazy, had it out for me. Tried to attack my wife once. I had his hands broken and called the cops on him. He got out, came back and tried to steal it again, the fuck. Somebody killed the spic a few weeks later."

"And I'm sure you had nothing to do with that, right?"

"Hey, I'm a business man, not a thug! And he wasn't worth the time. Just another dirty tortilla-munching Mexican. Like I said, maybe it's his grandkid or nephew or something?"

Time for the important stuff. Now I had to wonder who made the initial offer for this job: Old Man Ignorance, or the 1970's recording magnate still stuck inside his cracked head? I had a pretty good idea what his answer would be, but I had to ask.

"About the money, what you offered on the phone?"

The old man shifted in his bed, turning his eyes away from me and towards the door. Never a good sign.

"Look, Stetch...."

Then I saw what he was looking at: a tall, lithe redhead. I'm a sucker for redheads, just like Pops was. She had startling green eyes, and the greatest set of lips I'd ever seen on a woman—the bottom lip pouty and full, with a top lip just as welcoming and perfectly matched.

Chapter 2

She smiled as she stepped through the door, showing perfectly formed pearls of white between those red daydreams. Lush. That was the word for those lips. Or comfortable, like one of those overstuffed chairs that sucked your will to move the second you sat down. The woman looked to be around my age, his granddaughter, perhaps? God forbid it was his wife, though stranger pairings happened every day in California.

I hadn't seen at first from where I sat, but as I stood to welcome her, gentleman that Pops trained me to be, I noticed the girl. She was maybe six or seven, or she could have been four or twelve for all I knew about kids. She was cute, obviously the product of the lovely woman with the magic lips. The little girl had the same auburn tresses, the same green eyes. She'd be a heartbreaker someday, and a boatload of trouble, no doubt.

My gaze returned to the mother, who was leaning across the bed to hug the miserable old bigot I'd wasted my morning on, although I had to admit that the morning was looking up. It took me a second or two to realize that I was still standing, and staring, when the woman stood and held a hand out to me across the hospital bed.

"Hi. I'm Rose, Obie's daughter." The voice matched the lips. Pure velvet.

My knees buckled a little. "I... um... sorry. Cole, Moss Cole."

I reached out and shook her hand—soft and warm, welcoming. Her handshake was firm, not the frail laying-on of hand that a lot of women tended to do, as if they were Scarlett fucking O'Hara, afraid you'd break their delicate, dilettante fingers. This girl had confidence and character. I was doomed.

"My pleasure, Miss Stetch. I'm sorry, but you did say 'daughter'?"

It seemed patently ridiculous as she stood next to the withered old creep in the bed who, even in his heyday, could not possibly have contributed to the smouldering beauty from which I was currently trying to wrench my eyes.

I turned to the little girl, bowing with my hat in hand, hoping both to impress Rose Stetch and avoid making her uncomfortable with my schoolboy stare. "And you are?"

"Holly." She exuded the same confidence her mother showed. Yep, she'd be trouble by sixteen.

"Well, Holly, it is a pleasure to meet you. My name's Moss."

"Like on a tree? What kind of name is that?"

"Holly! Be polite," Rose warned.

I winked at Holly and stood to face her mother and grandfather. "It's all right. Kids will be kids, right?"

Rose smiled, her luscious lips turning up into something that made my pelvis vibrate and my heart echo in my chest. Sweat broke out on my forehead.

"Holly, honey, can you go wait in the hall for a minute? Go ask Nurse Terri for a cookie."

She turned and watched Holly skip out the door and down the hall, then turned back to me. The smile faded from her beautiful face, a look I knew well after many years of disappointing various women.

"Mr. Cole, my father is not interested in buying anything or investing in any businesses."

What? She thinks I'm a salesman? Gone was any semblance of cordial flirtation or even mild tolerance. Women tend to go that way around me, for some reason.

"Listen, I'm not—"

"Mr. Cole, this kind of thing happens all the time. I know Obie Stetch used to be a 'big-time operator,' or whatever you people call it, but he's just an old man now. He needs to be left alone."

The old man stiffened in his bed and shot her a look of pure vitriol. She recoiled like a kicked dog, and I again had the instant urge to smack Obie Stetch in the bald spot.

"Shut up, Rose," he said. "*I* called Cole. He's an investigator. He's gonna help me find the record."

She sank at the word *record*, and her exasperation made her look tired and worn. "We've been through this. It's gone. Let it go."

"This man can find it, and find whoever it is thinks they can fuck with Obie Stetch!"

The old prick clenched his fists in rage, and his glare burned a hole through the bare patch of wall where his record used to hang.

"Father—"

"I want you to give him a fucking check! It's still my money, Rose. You may have locked me up in this prison, but I am still the *man* in this family, goddamn it. I'm still your father!"

"But you—"

"I said write the fucking check!"

Rose looked from her father to me, her green eyes pleading, telling me everything I needed to know. Stetch couldn't really afford my services, and she wasn't about to let him try to pay, but she still wanted me to help the coot.

I hoped my eyes were communicating just as clearly: I was broke, needed the money and the work, and wasn't keen on helping the fucker even at full pay plus incidentals. I don't think we were simpatico.

"If you don't write that fucking check *right now*, I'll have Goldstein down here and cut you off so fast your pretty little red head will fucking *spin*!"

Rose flushed and glared down at her father. "*Fine*. But don't think for a second that you'll be staying with Holly and me if you can't pay for this place anymore."

Her father grunted and turned away like a spoiled child.

"How much are we talking about, Mr. Cole?"

The chill coming off her ran through me like a ghost. This one wasn't even my fault. I just got caught in the crossfire between a spoiled octogenarian and his fed-up daughter. I wanted no part of it, but needed the money. Of course, that didn't mean I couldn't play the good guy, right?

I shrugged good-naturedly and shifted on my feet in my best 'Aw shucks Ma'am' impression. "Well, I... we... discussed my normal rates, which would be five hundred for the consultation and fifteen hundred per week, but your father....'

She glared at me so hard it hurt my head. I guess she wasn't in the market for 'shucks.'

"How much, Mr. Cole?"

The way she said my name hurt even more than the glare. Watching it twist its way from between those beautiful lips through clenched teeth made me think of a ring-necked spitting cobra I'd met once in Mozambique. That had only been a slightly better morning than this.

"We don't have to," I stammered.

"My father is obviously a big boy and can do what he wants with his money, whether he has it or not. How much?"

Stetch broke in before I could undercut the deal.

"It's my fucking money. I told him I'd pay twenty-five grand to get the record back. Give him half. I gave more than that to that shithead Reagan for his campaign last year."

Rose Stetch looked as if she'd just been slapped by a ghost. "Twenty-five *thousand*? Are you insane? My *car* isn't worth that."

"Write the fucking check!' he screeched back.

She shot holes through my face with her blazing green eyes as she reached into the bag hanging from her shoulder. She looked down, shaking her head in anger just long enough to scribble something out, then tore the check from the book and thrust it across the bed at me. Stetch continued to stare at the wall like a sulking four-year-old.

I nodded to Rose and turned to her father on my way to the door. When I spoke, my voice croaked in a hushed whisper. "I'll check out your mysterious latin orderly and start contacting dealers and fences. I'll be in touch, Mr. Stetch."

They both stayed frozen, staring at ninety degrees from each other. Neither acknowledged my existence as I left. The acorn and the asshole tree.

I felt a little sheepish myself after that transaction. Now I was just a slimy, money-grubbing Dick-for-hire. How the hell had Pops done it? Endless tides of obnoxious assholes who thought they had a right to anything and everything they didn't already own. Jerk-offs like Obie Stetch making demands and treating you like an indentured servant. Covering up affairs and ruining business partners. Somehow, Pops used to avoid these jobs, but I have to pay the bills.

I shuffled down the hall to the nurses' station and asked the fat nurse if Enrique was around. She basically told me to go to hell, or the Human Resources department. Usually that's the same place. That dry, cottony feeling pulled at my throat, begging me to pour some whiskey down it, pleading with me to feed my stomach and my brain with the sweet, mind-numbing nectar of the gods, the one that used to drive all my troubles away. I thrust my hand into my pocket and found the coin, flipping it between my fingers in a desperate effort to shake the monkey off my back as a flop-sweat broke out on my forehead and behind my ears.

Holly came out of a common room at the end of the hall and waved as she saw me head toward the elevator. I gave her a little wave and flipped my hat up onto my head with a flourish and a bow. She giggled and bounced off to join the party. Nice kid. Too bad she'd end up like the rest of us.

Chapter 3

I stopped at the human resources department on my way out of the *FloHo Arms*. The woman at the desk was a big girl, but she wore it well, with a sly smile that suggested she wasn't hurting for attention. A quick smile and tip of the hat from me, and she gave me a peek at Enrique's file. Turned out his name wasn't Enrique. His name was Jorge Ramirez, and he was the only orderly who'd fit Stetch's description. She also gave me a peek at her pink XL panties as she bent in the most awkward way imaginable to get a file that was right in front of her. After having my libido kickstarted, then unceremoniously doused, by Rose Stetch, I can't say I was entirely uninterested.

I flirted long enough to find out that Enrique had given his notice right around the same time the record went missing. The file contained no mention of family or even an emergency contact, but there was an address in Van Nuys. The HR woman, Daphne, managed to offer that she could be found moonlighting as a latex-clad superheroine dominatrix named Lady Funbags. I couldn't deny my curiosity, but business called, and I was still stinging from being branded a thieving huckster by Rose Stetch and her magnificent lips.

I left the death house and marched straight across the street to a bar called the *Drum & Monkey*. Neither of those elements appeared in the décor of the dark, empty place, with plain square tables and an oak-top bar with about eighteen taps standing in the center. Gots'ta love a bar with taps. At just past noon, I had the place to myself. I got my coffee, and a shot of whiskey on the side, made some quick chitchat about the weather, and then took my drinks to sit by the window and keep my eyes laid out on the parking lot.

I'd barely sat down when Rose stomped out the front door of the home, practically dragging the poor kid Holly behind her. They got into a red Volvo and tore ass out of the parking lot. She was driving angry — justifiably so, I figured. Hard to imagine having that jerk-off for a father, let alone having to watch him squander what little money he probably had left... over a fucking record.

Oh well. Not my problem.

The bitter coffee had apparently been made in the same pot they washed rags in, so I took a couple of swallows, followed that with a big whiff of the shot glass, and left the whiskey and a five on the table. I was sorely tempted to drink the shot, but I was off the sauce. They called booze a liquid Devil for many a reason, and I'd been privy to every one of them.

I left the glass — and the whiskey — and set out to do some legwork. By the time I crept my way through noon-time traffic to the Hi-Lo Club, it was nearly two o'clock. My head ached from skipping lunch — and from obsessing over Rose Stetch and her majestic kisser. The sky had turned to a spotty, depressing gray smudge to match my mood. Something wasn't sitting right. It might have been the shitty dishwater coffee, or it might have been what Pops called the 'tingle,' that feeling that something didn't add up, even before you know what the numbers were.

***

The Hi-Lo was one of those ancient clubs where legends like Ornette Coleman, Miles Davis, even back to Duke and Basie, would come and hang out to jam in a nice quiet place. It was a tiny club for musicians, where good musicians came to listen to great ones.

I considered myself neither, but I knew some people.

The inside of the Hi-Lo was brightly lit this time of day, especially considering the dull smog covering the city outside. Light streamed in from high windows, giving the place an air of reverence and sacred power. A century of dust caught the sun in spotlights that swirled and twisted with the breeze. A lone gunman sat at the piano, tinkling out a little ragtime in pianissimo.

A burly dark giant of a man named Neville leaned behind the bar, towering over a newspaper. Charlie Moses sat in front of him on a stool, legs folded at the knee, with striped suit pants and suspenders — dapper as ever. He was humming some old Lula Reed tune and smoking a Pall Mall.

He'd started sending me out to get Pall Mall for him when I was six years old. Charlie had been my grandfather's best friend for fifty years, like an uncle to me. He also happened to be an encyclopaedia of local history, especially when it came to crime or jazz.

I sauntered up on his blind side and set myself quietly on the stool next to his, signalling Neville to play it cool. "Charlie Moses!" I yelled.

He jumped about three feet off the stool and landed, bent-knees shaking, facing me with his dukes up like Jack Johnson.

"Sweet thunderin' Christ, boy! You tryin' to gimme a heart attack?"

Then he laughed, that full, hearty and genuine laugh that had washed away whatever was wrong with life since I was a kid. Pops always said Charlie was the ugliest, blackest guardian angel he ever saw. Nobody was ever depressed or angry around Charlie, the antidote to all ailments.

He set himself back on the stool, refolded his legs and chuckled again, slapping me on the back and waving to Neville for another round. "Neville, set down a cup of joe for my boy, Mossy Moe."

He was still giggling and snorting when the drinks were set in front of us. "What you doing down here, Moss? Ain't you got a business to run now?"

"Always time for you, Charlie. Besides, I need a little history lesson."

He lit another cigarette and took a slug of his drink, Makers Mark on the rocks. He was from Watts, born and bred, but you would have sworn he was Southern gentility by the way he did everything—slow, calculated, full of pleasant ease and measured politeness. "More manners than the King of Siam," Pops used to say. Something else you never saw anymore—people with manners to spare.

"What's on your mind then, boy?"

"I took a job for Obie Stetch. You remember him from the old days?"

"No good sonofabitch. Screwed anything that moved and took cash. Especially liked to screw over the musicians in his clubs. His were the best to get noticed in and the worst to get paid at."

The guy at the piano moved into a steady rendition of *Misty*, and Neville took his paper to a corner table with a cup of coffee. I could smell the rum he put in it from across the room. The combination of smells made me hungry for jerk chicken.

"Stetch had a record stolen. Says it was Sinatra in '48, signed to him. He thinks it has something to do with some trumpet player he had bounced back then. Guy named Ramone?"

"Sinatra? Yeah, he was here in '48, played the Mozambique Club a couple of nights, did the Trocadero, then he went down to the Fillmore, hung out at the long bar for a couple of weeks. That was during the recording ban, so everybody was just kinda shufflin' round, playin' when they could. Frankie'd been the biggest game around, 'til '47. He got caught shakin' hands with that Mafioso Lucky Luciano. Then the papers started saying he was a communist. Then he went and got mixed up with that Lana Turner and left his wife and kids. By '48, they were sayin' he was done."

"If that was during a recording ban, how would Stetch have a record?"

"Well, guys like Stetch would have it set up to record in the club when one of the big boys came to town. He probably cut that in the club, then had a few pressed for friends or VIPs. Wouldn't have been able to sell it, though."

"You ever hear of this particular record? Sinatra at the Mozambique?"

While Charlie gathered his thoughts, I took a sip of my coffee. Not great. Needed some of Neville's rum. Still, I couldn't help but smile, feeling more comfortable than I'd been in weeks, just sitting here with ol' Charlie Moses.

Charlie had a habit of staring forward when he was deep in thought, stroking his goatee, then rolling his eyes up to the ceiling, followed by the rest of his head. His fingers would move down his throat and then he'd crack his neck to one side and.... Presto! He'd have it all figured out. I watched for the signs, and right on cue....

"Come to think of it," he said, straightening his head and pushing his glasses back up on the bridge of his nose, "that might have been the night Ella stepped in. The two of them tore that mother up! Something like three hours straight. Bud Powell sat in on piano, Lockjaw, Huey Long... and I think your boy Ramone would have been on the trumpet with the house band."

"Jesus Christ! Are you kidding me? Frank and Ella? You sure about that?"

"Shit yeah. I ever give you wrong before, Mossy Mo? Don't you question your elders. I'll whup your ass just like Moe would'a done. And don't fucking blaspheme in here."

I sat quiet for a moment, thinking about the angles on a piece of history like Frank Sinatra and Ella Fitzgerald on private wax. Why in the hell would Stetch keep something like that to himself? It would have been worth a small fortune.

I shook my head. "Frank and Ella never recorded together. I remember that. Pops told me about seeing them in Vegas, at Caesars in '74. He said he always wished they'd recorded together so I could have heard it. You know how crazy he was for Ella. If that was real, wouldn't Stetch have sold it?"

"Like I said, private recording. He wouldn't have been able to press it back then, on account of the ban. 'Course, he may have never told anybody and only cut one copy. Stetch was a nasty little number. He would have done it just to keep it from the rest of the world."

That made sense. From what I'd seen of Stetch, it would have been his greatest triumph to deny something like that to fans the world over, to bask in the glow that he alone controlled something so rare and desired.

"Wouldn't Sinatra have had something to say about it?"

Charlie let out a chuckle and scratched his chin.

"Boy, ain't no way Frank knew about that record, if there is a record. Frank hated ol' Obie Stetch. He was a foul man, a woman-hater, a miserly prick and, worst of all in Frank's blue eyes, a racist. Most every rich white man was back then—just the way of the world—but Frank was different. Look at Sammy Davis. Ain't nobody back then would have been real friends with some nigger soft-shoe hoofer. They paid him to dance and sing, sure, but they weren't about to sit down and eat at the same table. Frank, he loved ol' Smoke. Loved him like a brother and never treated him no different than he did anybody else. That was the mark of a real solid man back then."

I loved Charlie Moses like my own grandfather, so I tended to indulge his ramblings. Still, I needed info, so I tried to nudge him back on course.

"And what about Ramone? You remember what happened to him? Stetch gave me some line about him attacking his wife."

"Ramone. Yeah. Georgie Ramone. Hoarr-hey. He sure as shit wasn't no rapist. Ladies loved them some Georgie Ramone. He was like whatsisname, the silent movie fella... Valentino."

"So you don't think this Jorge would have attacked Mrs. Stetch?"

Charlie laughed. "Man, everybody knew about him and Mary Stetch. She was a gorgeous thing, making time on the side with Georgie. Hot and heavy, but consensual, y'know? Stetch found out, had him bounced. Hard. Way I heard it, they killed the poor bastard and left him out in the San Bruno Mountains. But that Mary Stetch.... Man. Whooeee! Looked like Rita Hayworth—red hair, green eyes, best set of lips you ever saw on a white woman."

"Yeah, I met the daughter today. Still having trouble walking straight."

"Daughter? She'd have to be old enough to be your mother, man. Mary Stetch went crazy, killed herself after Georgie Ramone disappeared. The daughter was maybe three or four at the time. That'd make her, what? 65? Shit. Send her my way. She be just right for old Charlie Moses."

"This daughter was my age, Charlie. But like you said... Rita Hayworth, magical lips."

"Grandaughter, maybe. Ain't no way that was Mary Stetch's little girl. Mary died in '48, just like Georgie Ramone."

"Sweet Jesus." I mumbled.

"Watch that mouth, boy."

My head was swimming with threads that didn't connect. Obviously Stetch was bullshitting me. Did I really care enough to chase it down? I had a check for a solid twelve Gs in my pocket, and all twelve of them were telling me to find the record and forget the rest. But where to start? If anybody knew what was on that record, it would be long gone, buried in some collector's stacks—some collector who would never admit what he had. If it was what Charlie thought it might be, it would be damned near priceless to some collectors, meaning gone, baby, gone.

I hammered down the rest of my cup-o-joe and slapped Charlie on the back. "Thanks, old-timer. You stay out of trouble."

"Where you goin'? Give ol' Charlie Moses a hug, now. You don't forget who you are, Moss Cole."

I pulled his spindly old frame to me and hugged him tight. I lifted him off the floor, then set him down and gave him a kiss on the cheek.

"See ya around, Charlie. Work to do."

He waved me off and turned back to his humming. I was almost out the door when he called after me.

"Cole! You be careful, boy. Obie Stetch is the kind of man hurt a lot of people in his life. I don't imagine one more would make any difference on his bill."

I winked and stepped back out into the bright afternoon.

Chapter 4

Stumbling out into the smog-filled afternoon, I was instantly blinded by the sun shining directly in my face. Or maybe that was just the effect of having somebody put a lead pipe across the back of my head with great force.

Probably the latter, since the next time my eyes forced their way open, I sat in a dank concrete room with no windows, full of busted old furniture, and two sweaty goons whose stench filled the air. Once I licked the marbles out of my mouth and confirmed my head was still attached, I addressed the two gentlemen who were doubtless responsible for tying me to the chair.

"Hey, fellas, any chance you'd want to untie me? This is kind of uncomfortable, y'know."

The big one turned and spit at my feet. "Shut the fuck up."

"All right then. One of you guys get me a cup of coffee? Bottle of water?"

Big boy was ugly, to be sure—big like a mountain, bald by choice, arms thick with muscle and ink, most of it Nazi regalia. He stomped forward and laid one of his big black boots right between my forcibly spread legs.

The momentum smashed my chair into the wall behind me, crushing my bound wrists and bouncing my already aching head on the concrete. Between the lightning storm crackling through my head, the throbbing ache in my hands and groin, and the lovely morning I'd spent dealing with senile dementia, I was having a Real Bad Day. But then, those came with the line of work.

As I sat moaning against the wall, Thug Number Two stepped up to the plate and had a couple of swings. He was blessedly smaller than his cohort—comically so—but with a backhand that could have smacked paint off a tank.

He at least had something to say between face-slaps. "Where's that fucking record, Private *Dick*?"

Slap.

"I said we want the record... *Dick*!"

Slap.

"You better talk... *Dick!*"

Slap.

As he beat a bongo tune on my face, I worked my arms until I had loosened the ropes almost enough to slip my swollen hands through. I hadn't yet thought of how to get my feet loose.

These two were hired goons—cheap, local muscle. No telling whom they were working for. When the little fella seemed like he'd tuckered himself out after four or five go-rounds, I spat out a mouthful of blood and corrected him.

"My name's not Dick."

Spit.

"So either you've got the wrong guy, or you are *not* the brains of the operation."

Spit.

The big boy decided it was his turn to play again, and roared forward as if he were defending the *Führer* himself.

I pulled my hands out from behind me, and half-cartwheeled to throw my still-bound knees and the chair they were tied to into his gut. The chair splintered and I was free, but the big Nazi was up fast, dragging me to my feet.

"Truce?" I winked. "I know some nice Jewish girls I could introduce you to."

He heaved me up to his eye level and growled like a lazy bear at the zoo.

"Black?"

Headbutt.

"Asian?"

Gut-shot.

"Hispanic?"

He tossed me like a rag doll over a heap of scrapped wooden chairs and table parts, into the corner of the room. As I struggled to my feet, he lumbered forward, hurling debris left and right like Godzilla clearing a path through downtown Tokyo.

I finally got my legs under me, and stopped my head from swimming long enough to find a thick mahogany table leg to defend myself with. I stepped forward with a hearty *have at you* just in time for him to slap the weapon out of my hand and wrap his Christmas ham-sized mitts around my comparatively tiny throat. I gasped and choked and gurgled, struggling to get loose, slapping at his bulky frame like a grade-schooler trying to get his lunch money back from a bully.

I mumbled a few unintelligible words and tried to look panicked.

He pulled me in closer to his face. "Whaddidyousay, fuckface?"

I had to strain to squeeze the words out of my cinched-shut throat, sounding something like Clint Eastwood with his head in a bucket of Texas barbecue sauce.

"I said... your... dick... is... out!"

He lost concentration and looked down, just for a heartbeat, but long enough for me to get my feet on the floor. I pistoned one boot-heel into the instep of his foot, then shot the same leg up and rammed my knee into his crotch. It connected hard enough to explode a testicle or two, but I wound up and planted a right hook on the side of his head, just to be sure.

The big man slumped in a heap of limp skinhead flesh.

I forced myself to stand, looking for his partner. It was the right thing to do, since Thug Number Two was behind me, swinging timber for the back of my favorite cranium. I stood just in time to take it in the shoulder. A white-hot explosion of new pain turned the room into a blinding sunspot for a second, but the arm still moved well enough to grab the little bastard and swing him around in a hip toss, landing him through a ramshackle pile of upturned furniture.

The air blasted out of his chest and he lay gulping for a breath.

I fell on my knees beside him and slapped his face to get his attention. "Hey! Breathe. Calm down, nice and slow. Breathe. Breathe."

With tears in his eyes, and clinging to my arm like a scared toddler, he gasped twice and managed to suck in a lungful. Not much of a tough guy—obviously the one to get answers from.

"All right, before I have to put you through another table.... What the hell is going on here?"

I laid a hard left to the side of his face, right around the orbital socket, where it would sting like a bastard and swell up fast.

"Who do you two geniuses work for?"

Before he could answer, the door opened behind me. I shot to my feet and whirled around, table leg back in my hand, ready for another round.

Two men stood backlit by the fluorescent glow from the hall, both well dressed in black suits—well-tended gentlemen with Italian shoes and manicured nails. These were thugs of a different stripe, the kind that used bullets to keep the blood off their cufflinks.

I clutched the table leg tight, and backed through the mess on the floor to stand in the middle of the room, leaving me space to maneuver.

The older of the two stepped forward and surveyed the landscape, shaking his head at the two goons lying prostrate on the floor.

"Joey, what the fuck is this? I told you to have the man picked up, not worked over. What is this, the fuckin' stone age? And what's with this fuckin' Nazi *finocchio*?"

The younger man stood his ground and took in the scene. He showed a respectful stoicism toward the older man, but his eyes flashed full of crazy — the kind of wild eyes you'd expect to see in a rabid wolverine, or a nightmare.

"Sorry, Mr. D," Joey replied. "Local strength. You know how these new by-laws are. We couldn't bring our own boys, so we had to use these L.A. *cazzos*." He shouted the insult and spat toward the kidnappers at his feet.

The older man navigated the debris to approach me. Upon reaching the open area in front of me, he carefully swept the legs of his pants and the arms of his impeccably tailored coat, straightened his tie, and looked me dead in the eye. "So you're Moe Rossi's boy?"

"Grandson."

"Grandson. Right. Mossimo, like him, right?"

"Yeah, but apparently you can call me Dick." I wiped blood from my eyes with the back of my hand, taking care to keep both men in my sights.

"Mossimo Cole, the McWop. You don't look much like the old man, kid."

"Sorry. You are?"

I was trying to be civil, desperate to be careful. These two had little in common with the brainless hoodlums on the floor. This pair was dangerous. Very dangerous.

He laughed, the calm relaxed laugh of a man assured there was no situation he couldn't handle. He shot his cuffs and bounced his head to one side in that stereotypical way that has become synonymous with Italian-American crime lords known as *Mafiosi*.

"Mossimo, my name is Tomaso DeFrancesco. You've heard of me?"

Chapter 5

Fuck me. My face must have betrayed the sinking feeling that took over the lower half of my body, pulling my swollen balls up to hide behind my spleen.

"Why don't you sit down, kid. I have to apologize for the way these *cazzos* treated you. Some people assume, because of my stature in certain circles, and because of my distinctly Italian heritage, that I expect these things to be done in my name. I assure you, I do not."

I knew who Tommy DeFrancesco was, all right, and wasn't about to contradict the man who killed half the Vegas mob or his buddy Joey "Thumbs" Testaverde, who would be the younger guy still standing in the doorway.

I took DeFrancesco's advice and pulled up a chair.

He also pulled up a chair and set it to face me. He took a handkerchief from his pants pocket and wiped the chair before sitting, gracefully, with his legs crossed and his hands folded in his lap. His charisma oozed from him like sweat, even sitting still in the middle of a basement junk drawer.

I looked nervously from DeFrancesco to Testaverde and back again. Thug Number Two had pulled himself up against the wall, where he sat head down, obviously hoping to blend into the concrete. The big skinhead just started to stir on the floor.

"You! Dickhead! Get up against the wall with your little friend," Testaverde commanded with a swift kick at the giant's exposed torso.

The skinhead complied without a word, crawling on his tree-trunk arms and legs until he too sat propped against the grey wall. He probably didn't understand Italian, but the message was pretty clear, regardless. Joey Thumbs stayed in the doorway.

I turned my attention back to DeFrancesco, who smiled amiably, watching me with mild curiosity.

"You really don't look like the old man," he said again, "but I can see some resemblance there. You certainly have his *coglioni*. You speak some *Italiano*? You know what I mean?"

I knew what he meant, even if his idea of Italiano consisted of spewing random profanities from every district from Valle d'Aosta to Sicily. I twisted uncomfortably on my swollen balls at the word.

"I do have abnormally large *coglioni* at the moment, thanks to Heinrich Himmler over there."

He laughed. "There it is! That's Moe Rossi through and through. I knew your grandfather, you know—a very good friend of my own father, Giusseppe DeFrancesco. They both came over from Torino in the old country, and grew up together in New York. Small world we live in, kid."

"Indeed it is, Mr. DeFrancesco."

"Please, kid, you call me Tommy. We're practically family here."

His kind of family I wanted no part of, but when in *Roma*....

"Sure, Tommy, so what brings me here?"

He kept the friendly face on, but I could see the calculation behind his eyes. He was the kind of man used to getting his way, at any cost. This called for caution—too much smartass and he'd wipe me from the face of the earth; not enough and he'd think I was hiding something. Then friendly Tommy would have his friend Joey Thumbs start breaking things, things I'd rather keep in one piece—didn't take a rocket scientist to guess that usually started with the thumbs.

"I've heard of a record," Tommy said. "A very rare record. A Sinatra record. I've also heard that you may know where to find it. Is this true?"

"I can't really talk about it. You know, client confidentiality and all that jazz."

Joey Thumbs stepped into the room.

"Watch your mouth, *fracicone*," he growled with a salacious grin, like he wanted to tear me open with his bare hands and make sweet love to my left ventricle.

Tommy looked back over his shoulder and waved Joey down, telling his dog to sit. "We're all friends here. *Famiglia*, all right? Just relax."

Tommy turned back to me, looking at me regretfully, as if to say, '*Sorry my hired thugs just beat the ever-loving shit out of you and possibly ruined your possibilities for future procreation.*' He finished his sensitive appraisal of my physical well-being and shook his head.

"Look, Mossimo, I understand. You don't feel like you can trust me. I'm supposed to be a notorious gangster. These men kidnap and beat you. You think I ordered that. You must feel like a prisoner."

"Actually it's been a lovely afternoon. I needed a workout." I wiped blood from my face with the back of my sleeve.

He glared to let me know he was losing patience. He was about to put the polite act back in the closet, in favor of something more comfortable.

Time to cut to the chase. "Look, Tommy, I don't know any more about it than you do. Less, probably. I'm guessing Stetch called you to help him find his record. One of his "friends," right? Well, the old man called me in to his sickbed this morning, told me a ridiculous story about how some kid at the hospital, name of Ramone, had something to do with it. The old guy is losing his mind. He wasn't making any goddamn sense. So I told him I'd look into it, and checked with the hospital—nobody named Ramone even works there. Turns out he was talking about some Mexican he shitcanned in the 40's. It's a fairytale, an old man's fever dream. Fuggedaboutit."

I may have overstepped my charm with the last comment, because Tommy reached across from his chair and backhanded me hard across the face.

"Watch that smart mouth. *T' Taggh' a facc', arruso. Capito*?"

Sure, I *capito*. He was going to fuck me in the ass. That was a threat. More than a threat, probably meant Joey Thumbs would do me with a shotgun or, if I was lucky, a baseball bat.

"No disrespect, Mr. DeFrancesco. I'm being totally honest with you. There *is* no record."

He stood and walked in a wide circle, until standing behind me, and placed his hands on my shoulders. All the better to intimidate me with. He leaned down and spoke quietly into my ear, his breath cool on my neck, which was still wet with blood from the back of my head.

"Oh, it's real, all right. And *you* are going to bring it to *me*."

He tightened his grip on my trapezius muscles, digging his fingers into the sensitive area above my collarbone. I winced and shrunk into my chair as he released my neck and stepped away from the chair, withdrawing his handkerchief again to wipe the blood from his fingers. He stood with his back to me for a moment, presumably gesturing to Joey Thumbs, who stepped back into the hallway and re-entered a second later with a briefcase.

I hoped to Christ it was their idea of a bag lunch.

DeFrancesco sat back in the chair, comfortable as could be, quietly re-crossing his legs and smoothing the pleat of his pants, and Testaverde came to stand beside him with the case.

"I first met your grandfather in 1974 at Caesar's Palace. He sat with my father and me as we watched Sinatra and Miss Ella Fitzgerald perform on stage. I liked Moe Rossi, a good man, and a good friend to my father. You? So far? I could live without. So be careful and listen. Keep your smart mouth shut, hmm?"

I sat arrow-straight and rigid against the back of the chair. It's a fact. I could be a mite obnoxious at times, a curse I'd have to live with — if I managed to live much longer.

"Your grandfather told me a story that evening, of how he first met Sinatra in 1948, when he helped him to deal with some blackmail issues over his affair with the actress Lana Turner. He told me how he had seen Ol' Blue Eyes sing at the Trocadero, and at the Long Bar in Fillmore. He also told me that Frank and Ella had performed together during that same time, at a place called The Mozambique Club, and that Mr. Obie Stetch apparently had the only copy of the only recording ever made of the two performing together. Now, you tell me, Mr. Cole, are you calling your own beloved grandfather a liar? Because I met Sinatra that night in '74, saw him embrace your grandfather as an old friend, and I watched them drink and laugh and talk for hours. Your grandfather was a respected man. You? You're nothing."

I must have looked ridiculous, covered in blood and sweat, face swollen and bruised, frozen like a mannequin with my jaw resting at my feet. Pops had never told me about the record, but he had told me about seeing Sinatra at Caesar's with some 'old friends.'

"I thought that might open your mind a little," DeFrancesco continued. "I am a reasonable man, Cole. I've been trying to acquire this particular record most of my life. You may or may not know that I have a sizable collection of Sinatra recordings and memorabilia — call it a hobby — and I would very much like to own this piece. I am a man who gets what he wants, Cole. "

He gestured back to Testaverde, who set the case on his boss's lap as if he was laying a napkin for dinner. He snapped open the clasps and flipped the lid. It was full of lettuce, the nice kind that comes with pictures of presidents on it.

"This is fifty thousand dollars, Mr. Cole. I am prepared to pay that much for the pleasure of owning this particular item. If you were to deliver it to me, I would be graciously indebted to you. *A capito?*"

"Yeah, I *capito.* But what if I don't find it?"

Joey Thumbs reached down to snap the case shut and set it next to the chair while Tommy shrugged my question off.

"Hey! You don't find it, you don't find it. We all go back to our lives and I keep searching on my own. But I would be greatly dismayed if I found out that you disrespected my wishes."

I eyeballed the case, then looked at Joey Thumbs, who was staring a hole through my forehead, no doubt hoping to take a few more pints of blood out of me before they left.

Then I looked at Tommy. "So what you're really asking me is, if I find the record, to make sure you get it."

"That's all." He smiled like a man with a knife behind his back.

"If I do, I'm fifty grand richer with no strings attached?"

"Exactly."

"And if I find it, but don't hand it over to you, Joey Thumbs here stomps a mudhole in my brainpan, I'd imagine?"

Tommy turned red. Joey Thumbs lunged forward, but the boss stopped him just short of my face. "Joey, relax."

The pitbull jabbed a finger in my forehead and his eyes glowed with mad fury. He shouted in my face, spittle and psychopathic anger splattering off my face. "Watch your fucking mouth, you mick half-breed fuck! I'd be happy to put a bullet in that smart fuckin' face of yours."

"What are you mad at me for, Joe? I didn't knock up your mother."

The place went white again as Thumbs popped me a short but practised jab right between the eyes. A warm gush of blood flowed like a waterfall down my face.

"Joey, that's enough." DeFrancesco put on the voice.

Testaverde backed away, rubbing his knuckles until he was standing next to the boss. I was hoping he cracked at least one of them on my face.

Tommy stood, straightened, buttoned his jacket and threw his handkerchief at me. "I hope you're just having an off day, kid. That mouth is going to get you in real trouble one of these days."

"I thought getting kidnapped and braced by the mob would be trouble enough."

He laughed in a quick snort, then shot his cuffs again as he turned to walk away.

"Just bring me the record, Cole."

"Hail Caesar."

He laughed as he stood and carefully dusted his sleeves again.

Joey Thumbs stayed put, inches away, staring intently into my face with the glowing eyes of a rabid animal.

I sucked up a mouthful of blood and spat a wad at his feet. "Go fuck yourself, Joey." I stared calmly into his reddening face.

DeFrancesco was at the door, waiting, shaking his head in disgust. He called off his dog before he could take another nip at me.

"Joey, make sure these two *tarzanellos* take him back in one piece. Nothing happens to him unless I say so."

"Sure, Mr. D." He smiled down at me with what could only be called murderous glee, then stepped around a few piles of junk and clapped the little guy in the side of the head.

"You hear that, you fuckin' hump? Take him back where you got him, and no more playtime, or you answer to me. *Got it*?"

He looked them both up and down, then stepped to the door as Tomaso DeFrancesco headed down the hallway.

"Hey, Joey!" I called after him, coughing through a little blood and a lot of pain. "Say hi to your mother for me."

He turned, silhouetted and framed by the door, and cocked his finger at me like a kid playing Cowboys and Indians. "Click, click, motherfucker." He laughed and disappeared.

I'd have to remember to send him a nice "Welcome to Sunny L.A." package, courtesy of the ol' Hat Squad. Detectives Lincoln and McGuire of the Organized Crimes Department would be very interested to know the mob was in town.

I spat again and looked over at Tweedledum and Tweedle Reichstag.

"So, you guys ready to go?"

Chapter 6

Ten minutes later, I was back in the car that had brought me to my afternoon meet n' greet with the Vegas mob. It turned out to be a beat-to-shit mid-'80s Monte Carlo with a charming half shit-brown, half rust, two-tone paint job. I'd probably need a tetanus shot just for standing next to it. At least this time I was propped-up in the backseat, more or less under my own control.

The big skinhead drove and the little thug rode shotgun. They nervously ignored me for the first twenty minutes of the drive. Buck Owens, of all things, garbled his way through the tinny speakers behind my still ringing ears.

"Look, guys, no hard feelings, huh? I'm pretty sure I got the worst of it. Forgive and forget. That's my motto."

The Nazi half-turned from the steering wheel and tried to point a threatening finger my way. "I ain't fucking talking to *you*!"

The little guy put his hand on Himmler's arm—sensitively, like a mother. Or a lover. "Settle down, Yergs."

"Yergs?" I asked.

The little guy jerked his head my way, aggravated by my intrusion on their moment. "Yeah, his name is Jurgen. Any more questions, Dick?"

"Again with 'Dick?' Really?" I coughed out a small clot of blood and flicked it at the grimy floorboard. "Come on, man. We don't have to be enemies just because you guys got paid to rough me up a bit, do we? Seems to me, we both ended up on their bad side pretty handily."

It never hurts to have connections. Pops taught me that one too. Make friends with both sides of the fence.

"My name's Cole. Moss Cole."

"Yeah. Mossimo, right? You're a fucking *guido* like those two," Jurgen barked back.

"Half right. My grandfather was Italian. I'm half Irish too. And all Californian. Want to take a stab at that race, Yergy?"

He eyed me in the rear-view mirror.

I smirked at the reflection of the bruised face and bloodshot eye, where I'd knocked him on his giant racist ass.

"Fuck you," he said, matter-of-fact.

"What about you, pal?" I asked his partner. "You a racist *schweinhund* like your boyfriend?"

That got their attention. Jurgen immediately stiffened in his seat and the little guy gasped despite himself. He paused for a second and then whipped around to face me. "What the fuck did you just say?"

I looked him dead in the eye and smiled—as much as I could smile, what with half my face swollen shut. Even half-conscious, I was a perceptive son-of-a-bitch.

"Why hide it? You two are together, right? I'm not judging you." I looked at Jurgen in the rear-view, trying to avoid looking back. "But Yergy, you should know that homosexuals were branded inhuman, same as Jews."

I just barely caught the little fella's reaction through the blurry corner of my eye.

"And you," I said, mildly surprised, "you're Jewish."

Magnificent! It wasn't every day I had a free-for-all rumble with a gay Nazi and his Jewish lover. That was one for the books—a new one for me, anyway.

He turned back to the front seat and stared at Yergy with what looked like regret. "He's not really like that."

Holy shit! Now I was stuck in the middle of a movie on the Lifetime network.

"All right." I offered as understanding and apologetic a tone as I could muster. "Let's start over, guys."

I shifted myself over with no small amount of discomfort and stuck my head up between the seats.

"Hi, my name's Moss Cole." I stuck my hand out.

Yergy glanced down at it as if I'd offered him a dead puppy, then looked up at his partner with an expression of utter confusion.

The little guy, in turn, studied my face for a long second, then shook the hand. "Menlowe. My name is Arthur Menlowe. This is Jurgen Kierkedoek."

I started to laugh, and fell back against the seat coughing and writhing in pain.

"What's so funny, motherfucker?" Jurgen roared from the driver's seat, stretching to glare at me in the mirror.

I caught my breath and wiped a tear from my tender face.

"I know who you guys are. Kickerdick and Manlove, right? I knew I'd seen that big ugly head somewhere before. You guys do gay bondage porn!"

"We prefer to call it *fantasy enactment*. Why? Are you a fan, sweetheart?" Menlowe let his faux-Bronx accent melt into soft Orange County fluff.

"Lord no!" I coughed. "Not that it wasn't... umm, entertaining? Just not my thing."

I laughed again and felt something grinding around in my side, something very uncomfortable, something like a broken rib. I was having a hard time holding in my bladder, not that anyone would have noticed in that backseat.

"I had a divorce job a year or so ago. Guy turned out to be a closet job. No offense. He was heavy into your stuff. I tailed him to one of your shows in the valley. He had a stack of your DVDs. Holy shit!" I laughed my ass off at how ridiculous it was, like some Coen Brothers movie come to life.

"Quit fucking laughing!" hollered Kickerdick.

"Okay, okay, I'm sorry." I paused to catch my breath.

Manlove rested his chin on the seat and watched me with curiosity. "So you follow people around and wreck their marriages? And steal records for the mob?"

He had a good point, but it wasn't anything I hadn't already put myself through the ringer for. A million times over. Didn't mean I was going to let an insult stand unchallenged.

"Well, you guys fuck each other in chainmail in front of bored executives and tortured schoolteachers."

Also a good point, I thought.

Manlove shrugged. "But we don't hurt anybody, really. That's all an act. You break up families and steal from old men."

I let my head loll back to rest on the top of the seat, Buck Owens caterwauling in my ears. "It *is* a shitty job, I'll give you that. But all I really do is get proof of the awful things people are already doing."

"And that absolves you somehow? You must be a fucking Catholic." He waved a hand in dismissal and turned back to stare at the oncoming traffic.

Again, nothing I hadn't pondered for myself. Reason #236 I'd quit drinking: it led to wallowing in my own misery over a job that constantly pushed the bounds of comfortable morality. My jobs usually ended with somebody getting their life fucked up.

I took a breath and decided to let it go. "So what's with the ink then, Kickerdick?" I flopped forward faster than I'd meant to, and caught myself just before falling face-first into the stick shift.

He gave me what I had come to understand was his standard *hard-ass* look, but it seemed to fade into amusement when I grimaced in pain after he put the car in a pothole.

I'd almost given up on polite conversation when he finally answered. "I was a stupid kid. Now they're just good for getting people to leave me alone."

Manlove reached past me to take Kickerdick's hand.

How the fuck had I ended up in this position? I really need to find a new line of work. I was either getting my ass handed to me by giant skinheads and mob enforcers, or sitting front-row on Springer.

"Well, I guess it works for your show, right? You guys are all right. I'm sorry I kneed you in the balls."

He looked down at my battered face and smiled. "Yeah, all right. Sorry I whupped your ass like a schoolgirl."

I laughed again, which was becoming a serious problem, pain-wise. "Okay, big boy, I'll give you that."

I realized we were only two or three blocks from my place, and if we went all the way back to the Hi-Lo, I'd have another half-hour drive to get back home.

"You guys mind dropping me off a couple blocks from here?"

Manlove smiled sweetly and nodded. "Sure, Cole."

Chapter 7

Soon I was slowly extracting myself from the back seat like a broken folding chair.

Manlove leaned over Kickerdick and blew me a kiss. "See you, sweetie."

I think I rolled my eyes—hard to tell, since everything above my jawline was numb. It probably looked more like I was blinking out Morse code.

Kickerdick hung a giant tattooed arm out the window and levelled it at me like a shotgun. "Not a word. Right?"

I nodded and slapped the roof of the car. "Not a word, Mr. Kierkedoek. Not a word."

I stumbled off with a wave, stuffing a business card for "Manlove & Kickerdick" into my pocket and praying for death.

The sun had already set on the clear evening as I stumbled my way toward the front step of my building. The streetlights had just come on, and through my cloudy eyes, they looked like stars floating around me. As I got closer to the door, I could make out the shape of someone leaning against the entrance, someone tall and red.

"What the hell happened to you?" She rushed down the steps towards me, and bobbed around me for a second trying to survey the damage. Then she wove a long slender arm under my throbbing shoulder and around my back.

I winced as my arm came up to give her access. "Just meeting with potential customers." My eyes watered from the pain. "To what do I owe this pleasure, Miss Stetch?"

"Jesus! Let's get you inside. Where are your keys?"

"Front pocket, next to what's left of my spleen."

She gingerly fed her hand into my pocket and felt around until she fished out the keys.

"I'll be honest. That was the very best part of my day so far." I coughed.

She shushed me and fumbled to fit the security key into the lock.

The two of us wrestled my remains up the stairs, with more than a few shouted curses and high-pitched squeals on my part. The neighbors were probably imagining someone actively forcing a live hog up the stairs by means of cattle prod.

Once she'd managed to tumble me into my apartment, she helped me to the couch, laid me back, pulled off my boots, and lifted my feet to stretch out my legs. I hadn't enjoyed such favorable attention from a woman in months.

"Can I get you anything?" she asked. "Water? Should I call a doctor?"

She was especially cute when panicked and concerned. The excitement brought a flush to her cheeks that gave faint accent to those fantastic lips.

"I'm okay," I replied, despite finally feeling the extent of my bruising all at once. "I *have* spent all day praying for a decent cup of coffee."

A few seconds later she was rustling around the kitchen, clinking glasses, opening the freezer door looking for ice. She muttered, then smashed something against the counter.

Eventually she hustled back into the room, struggling with two large bags of frozen vegetables. "I didn't see an ice pack or anything. Here."

She shoved me over, almost burying my face in the back of the cushions, and jammed one of the bags under my neck and head, which made me feel about equivalent to the underside of the Titanic. No sooner had the stars stopped blasting into my eyeballs than she grabbed me by the shoulders and slapped my torso back onto the couch. I howled as the cold hit my neck, and the jagged wound I was sure bisected the back of my skull.

"Sorry! Sorry! Guess I'm not much of a Florence Nightingale."

The ice pillow started to work its magic, and the pain subsided, leaving me almost euphoric with relief. "You've been wonderful. Thank you, Rose."

"Call me Rosie. Everybody but my father calls me Rosie."

"Rosie, then. Thank you, Rosie." I smiled weakly and began to reach for her hand when spasms tore into my shoulder, causing my arm to recoil and glue itself to my side. "Fuhhhhuhuhuhuk me!"

"Oh, God! Umm, what is it? What—oh God, what do I do? What *can* I do? Here!"

She thrust the other bag at me—peas, I think. Whatever they were, they were solid as concrete and felt twice as comfy jammed into my damaged ribs, which elicited a girlish scream.

"Sorry! Sorry! Oh God. I'm so sorry!"

My cries for mercy were interrupted by a harsh thumping on my door.

"What the hell is going on in there? Mossimo Cole, you open this door right now, young man!"

Mrs. Bradley—nosy neighbor, incorrigible busybody, world-class gossip, and my landlady. She also made a mean mac-and-cheese casserole and frequently brewed homemade beer—a brew that smelled like death and tasted, I could only imagine, like the inside of a goat's ass.

Rosie, flustered, hovered between the couch and the door, not sure which to deal with first. After a few seconds' hesitation she opened the door a crack, just enough to let Mrs. Bradley shove past and into the middle of my living room.

The old lady glared at me with incredulous aggravation.

"Jesus H. Christ, Moss. What the hell did you get yourself into now? Let's have a look at you."

Mrs. Bradley had been an army nurse in Korea and was usually good for a couple of stitches or setting fingers and noses. She was even rougher than Rosie. As had usually been the case, the women in my life were fairly unconcerned with my discomfort.

"Christ almighty, boy!" She shoved me back on my side, where I found myself suffocating in my own sofa cushions once again.

"This smack on your head needs stitches. Looks like you broke your nose again, maybe a couple of ribs."

She flopped me back to prone and then hauled me up to sitting, which did nothing for my appreciation of her bedside manner.

"Come here, honey," she said to Rose. "Help me get his shirt off."

They wrestled me out of my shirt with some protracted pushing and pulling. I felt self-conscious with Rosie there, staring at my scar- and tattoo-riddled body, mangled and bruised as it was. Not the best impression I could make on a young lady. I tried to keep my shirt clutched to my chest, but Mrs. Bradley pulled it from my grasp as she poked and shoved and felt around my back and my bruised sides.

"Take a breath," she demanded.

I took a shallow suck of air that felt like I was trying to stuff a Volkswagen into my chest.

"A deep breath, stupid!" She smacked one of the bruises.

I took as deep a breath as I could muster, and my head swam as the Volkswagen morphed into a Greyhound bus.

"Where else?" She stood with hands on hips and a suspicious glare on her pudgy, wrinkled face.

My balls were still aching but, thankfully, in a dull, far-off way, compared to everything else. I wasn't about to go whipping my swollen nads out for the room to examine in detail.

"My shoulder took a little carpentry lesson."

"I can see that. Twelve shades of bruised already. Might be dislocated, probably fractured. You'll have to see a real doctor for that one, but we can keep it out of your way for now." She paused, then poked me hard in the back. "Is that another goddamn tattoo? What are you doing to yourself, Cole? You might as well join a damn carnival. What the hell would your grandfather say if he saw you like this? Did that Danny Fox get you in trouble again?"

It was the voice of a disapproving mother, grilling a soon-to-be-grounded eight-year-old for information. *Who taught you that horrible word? What kind of an idiot? Where did you get naked pictures of the neighbor girl?*

"I haven't seen Danny in months."

"Well, he was by here this afternoon, rolled up in a limo, screaming at the top of his lungs and throwing beer bottles at your window."

"Christ."

"I chased him off fast enough. You keep that no-good punk away from my building." She turned and looked Rose over, top to bottom. "Did *you* get him into this kind of trouble?"

Rose was taken aback.

I twisted myself enough to see them, and called Bradley off before she got the wrong idea. "She's a client. A different client," I explained. "She just happened to find me on the front stoop."

Mrs. Bradley finished her appraisal of the tall redhead and looked back at me over the top of her glasses. "Stay put. I'll be right back."

Chapter 8

Rose sat down on the edge of the couch and began to run her fingers through my hair.

I was in heaven. "So why are you here? Not that I mind in the least bit."

I pushed my eyes as far back as they would go, which was not far at all, tilting my head against the melting vegetables to look up at her with as much *puppy-dog* as I could manage.

She looked troubled, but still absolutely stunning. "I wanted to ask you to reconsider. My father is starting to get—"

"Senile?"

She looked down at me with her brilliant green eyes and nodded. "He doesn't have the kind of money he's promised you."

"He would if he had that record."

She studied me with a look of suspicion. "What do you mean? How?"

I propped myself up on my elbows, despite the screeching stab of pain that ran through my shoulder.

"How do you think this happened?" I pointed at my face. "A couple of goons shanghaied me for a Vegas mobster named Tommy DeFrancesco, who happens to style himself the world's biggest Sinatra fan."

"I thought they got rid of all the mobsters in Las Vegas."

I laughed, then curled half in a ball from the ensuing blast of molten lava running through my side.

"Don't believe everything you hear on the local news, honey," I replied. "Wherever there's money to be had and desperate people to steal it from, you'll find shady characters like DeFrancesco. He says he'll pay me fifty grand for the record if I find it. He also says he'll have me chopped up and put in a risotto if I give it back to your father. So I guess this is what's called a lucky break."

"So, what? You won't take our money?" She looked surprised.

"Look, Rosie, if I take your money, I have to find the record and give it back to your old man. I do that, and a guy named Joey Thumbs is going to embalm me while I watch."

"But my father—"

"Your father what? I'm not sure I want to do business with him anyway. I've heard some pretty unflattering stories today, and he's more or less out of his fucking mind, am I right? Besides, I thought you came here to talk me out of taking the job?"

Her face flushed, and she turned away from me and....

"You're kidding, right? You're crying now? I already said I wasn't going to take the money. Do you care about that miserable old prick that much? Or did he send you to sweet talk me into doing it for free? Or did he tell you to do more than talk?"

"Please, don't—"

"I wouldn't put it past him from what I've heard. He's not such an angel, your father. The man he was talking about—Ramone? From what I hear, Daddy had him beaten, probably killed, for screwing around with his wife."

"Don't you ever talk about my mother!"

I could hear the arctic freeze in her voice, but struggled to sit up and get a better angle on her reactions.

"Couldn't have been your mother, honey. This was in 1948, which would make you at least sixty."

The colour drained from every part of her, including those luscious lips. Even her green eyes seemed to turn grey. Her shocked expression showed that she had no idea what I was talking about. She sat down hard on the edge of the table.

"Who told you that?"

"A very old friend with a memory like an elephant, the kind I trust with my miserable life. He was around in the old days when your father ran his clubs. He knew the wife. Her name was Mary. She had a fling with a trumpet player named Jorge Ramone. Obie found out about it and had some muscle put on the guy. The story goes, they took him all the way out to San Mateo, busted his hands up, beat him, and dumped him in the woods on San Bruno Mountain. Nobody ever saw him again. Your father was practically bragging about it this morning."

She stood frozen, and the wheels moved at light speed behind her Irish eyes. "No, no. Dad would never—he's crazy. He doesn't even know his own name some days. He never had another wife."

"Mary Stetch killed herself a few months later when she heard what had happened to her lover. Pills. They had a little girl who was maybe four or five years old. You don't have a much older half-sister? What about your mother? Where is she?"

She got up abruptly and walked to the middle of the room, keeping her back to me.

That had been happening a lot lately. I was getting tired of talking to backs and asses.

"My mother died when I was only a few months old." Her voice was flat and lifeless. "I'm not here to talk about my mother."

"Rosie—"

"I know my father has done terrible things. That he's... he was a bad man to a lot of people."

"I'm sorry. I was just trying to explain."

She turned and wiped tears from her eyes, sobbing, trying to laugh it off in that nervous way women have when they don't want you to know how upset they really are. She looked like a hurt little girl.

I could see how even a certified bastard like Obie Stetch could have been moved to change his stripes enough to take care of her. Despite my battered, stiff and bloodstained frame, I desperately wanted to hold her, console her, be the one to make everything all better. I tended to be a sucker like that.

I was just ramping up the courage to drag my ass off the couch when Mrs. Bradley came back through the door with an armload of bandages and wraps, and a big bottle of hooch. It might have been whiskey. Then again, knowing Mrs. Bradley, it might have been lighter fluid and 7-Up.

Rose took the bottle and quick-stepped into the kitchen, wiping her face on her sleeve, shouting back that she was getting us a drink.

Mrs. Bradley gave a cursory glance at me struggling to get up off the couch, then leaned over to peer at Rose. She turned back, shoved me back into the upholstery, and shook her head. "You should be ashamed, upsetting that poor girl. You are a dog, Mossimo Cole, just like your grandfather was."

She always got a twitch at the corner of her mouth, and a wet couple of eyes when she talked about Pops. She had a torch burning for the old man, but he'd never given her the tumble she was waiting for.

"Stand up. This'll be easier that way." She had a way of talking until you just kind of surrendered to it and followed orders.

Mrs. Bradley placed her supplies on the coffee table and shook out a blue bedsheet. She waved Rose over as she entered the room, gesturing for her to take the other end. They twisted the sheet into a quick rope of loose cotton.

"Now tie that end in a knot, sweetie."

I wasn't sure what purpose their makeshift hank would serve, but Mrs. Bradley centered it under the armpit of my purple side and twisted it around the outside of my upper arm. She knotted it and handed the loose ends to Rose, then shoved and kneaded my shoulder. It screamed bloody murder straight into my brainpan every time she touched it.

"Okay, kid. This is gonna smart. I know you swore it off, but you're gonna want to take that drink." She nodded for Rosie to feed me one of the glasses of what turned out to be somebody's definition of scotch. She took the bedsheet back from Rosie, wrapped the ends around her wrists for purchase, and took a step back.

I realized what she was planning just in time to steel myself for what was coming. It wouldn't be the first time I'd felt the brutal "healing" hands of Ethel Bradley. I gave in and tossed the glass of amber sunshine down my gullet with a twinge of regret and an unhealthy dose of giddy anticipation.

I'd barely felt the burn hit my stomach before Mrs. Bradley knocked the wind out of me, planting a foot in my side and yarding back on the sheet hard enough to give me whiplash. After a godawful *pop*, my head swam in white light again. Those funny old stars filled my eyes, and the room spun like a full-tilt carousel.

She let me go and I crumpled to the floor. Rose caught me just before a perfectly good coffee table dented my cranium.

It took a second for me to catch my breath, and to let the tears clear out of my eyes, before I realized that I could move my arm. I gave it a very tender over-the-top stretch—painful, but workable.

"You still want to get that checked for a break, Cole, but at least it's back where it's meant to be."

I eased back onto the couch, suddenly feeling a little lightheaded, and Rose sat with her fingers pressing into my thigh, which did nothing to improve the amount of blood flow above my shoulders. I stared into her mesmerizing emerald eyes, occasionally losing myself between those juicy lips, barely noticing as Mrs. Bradley sewed the back of my head back together. The looks I was getting back made the ache in my balls recede to a dull roar, as every ounce of energy flittered forward to stand the ol' main-mast at attention.

Her sly smile showed the tiniest bit of those pearly whites, beneath a little coquettish eyelash flutter.

If I hadn't been so completely knackered, I probably would have questioned her timing. I mean, she couldn't stand the sight of me earlier in the day, and now she was making with the come-hither? At the time, however, I was happy just to stare at her and daydream about the color of her panties.

We were rudely and abruptly interrupted in our quiet flirtation by Mrs. Bradley shoving a couple of expired Percocets into my hand, blocking Rosie from view with the stern face of a pissed-off grandma, shaking a pudgy finger in my face.

"If you weren't already so beat up, Cole, I'd kick your little ass myself. This is getting to be a dangerous goddamn habit, young man. I'll be up to check on you later." She bundled up her supplies in the bedsheet and turned to Rose. "Don't you let him have any more booze, and leave the door unlocked when you go, okay?"

"Do you think he'll be all right?" Rose asked, seeming genuinely concerned.

"He's beat to shit. Definitely has a concussion. I'll need to check up on him a couple times tonight." She looked Rose up and down. "Unless you're planning on staying the night?"

Rose looked over towards me, contemplating something. She hesitated, unsure, and when she finally answered, it was barely a whisper, and her cheeks flushed. "I'll stay with him for a little while. If that's all right?"

Mrs. Bradley threw me another of her patented disapproving glares, then gave a *harrumph* and looked Rose over once more. "Well, I guess he can't cause too much trouble tonight... but *no funny stuff*." She stabbed a gnarled finger in my direction.

I tried to look innocent. It obviously had a diminished effect in my bruised and battered condition. She wasn't buying a thing, which didn't really matter. The thought of any *funny stuff* in my current condition, regardless of Rosie Stetch's charms, or the throbbing in my jockeys, was utterly ludicrous.

"I'll be back in the morning. I don't want any more goddamn noise!"

To Rose she gave a wink and added, "Don't kid yourself, Red. This one is all kinds of trouble in a handsome little package."

With that, Mrs. Bradley left, and Rose locked the door a few seconds later. She crossed the room and gazed out the window at the front lawn where she had found me. She hugged her arms to herself as if cold, despite the sweltering heat of the apartment.

"Does this kind of thing happen a lot? Getting kidnapped and beat up?"

"Occupational hazard," I grumbled, twisting to get comfortable. "I did all right for myself this time."

She gazed back at me with a sour look of disbelief.

"But, yeah, I've had my ass kicked more often than not." I tried to laugh, but even those muscles failed me as the percs kicked in.

She closed the curtain, walked slowly to the table for her drink, and stood looking at me with a very sad expression that made my chest hurt—like the face a mother gave when you were sick with a 110-degree fever.

"He wasn't really even a good father, y'know? But he was all I had, and now I have to return the favor, right?"

I had no idea where in the hell that came from, but she was choking back tears again, breaking my heart with each wet little diamond rolling down her perfect cheeks. I struggled to keep my thoughts straight and my mouth working through the fog that was creeping over my brain.

"Look, Rosie, I like to think I'm a decent guy. I'm not taking your father's money, all right? Life's too short. And it'll be real short if I start double-crossing sociopaths like DeFresca and Thumbsy Joe." I shook my head, trying to loosen the cobwebs as my mouth filled with marbles.

She smiled, but it was forced and unsure, and not at all worthy of that face. It hardly cut through the tears. She could tell how buggered I was, but she just kept talking.

I wanted to explain myself, but the connection was shutting down between my drugged and swollen brain, and my bruised and battered lips.

"Hhhunnnesteee, it's note a bug deeelll," I slurred, twisting and shifting myself around, trying to get my hand into the front pocket of my pants to extract the check she had given me that afternoon.

What I managed was to roll half on my shoulder, yelp in pain, twist back the other way, and then slip off the couch and crash onto the floor on top of my banged-up side. I howled into the carpet and lay there helpless on the floor.

She dropped to her knees beside me, close enough for me to feel her breath as she got her delicate hands under my arms, helped pull me up to sitting, and then up to my feet. Unfortunately, the legs above them had punched out and gone home for the night. She was obviously well aware of it, because she slid under my good arm and held me up in the blink of an eye.

"Come on. Let's get you to bed," she purred.

She walked me back to my room with no small amount of difficulty. Still, despite my useless and barely conscious condition, certain parts of my anatomy were wide awake and screaming for attention. It wasn't often that I had a smoking-hot redhead leading me to the bedroom. Not lately.

"Is that your grandfather?" She pointed at a picture on the wall—me and Pops at my Police Academy graduation.

Me: fifteen years younger, fifteen pounds lighter, built like a boxer, all squares and bundles of muscle. Pops stood next to me: tall, dark, and undeniably handsome, even as a very old and sick man.

My brain slipped away from me, jumbling images and memories, melting sounds from that day with the slowly dissolving picture of Rosie Stetch and her magical lips. Lips that were growing and twisting and distorting as they moved, two bright red snakes slithering across a marble floor.

I was vaguely aware of a mumbling voice, not unlike my own, as I reached out to the very shapely looking shadow in front of me. Then I was falling backward, down and down into a long black pit of silence.

Chapter 9

I woke to the sound of music. It was Sinatra.

"SOME PEOPLE GET THEIR KICKS STOMPIN' ON A DREAM...."

I tightened my gut and was painfully reminded of the ass-kicking I'd been dealt. I winced while feeling around my face and ribs, masochistically poking at bruises. I swung my legs out and stood up, weak and wobbling, but still in one piece, and still wearing my pants, but no shirt. I knelt down and reached under the mattress for the .22 I kept for mysterious visitors, especially ones who loved Sinatra. I didn't intend to be such an easy target this time.

I moved carefully out of the bedroom, pistol down and away like they teach you in cop school. The living room was clear, but sounds indicated someone moving around in the kitchen. I made my way as quietly as possible to the kitchen door, careful to avoid brushing my battered ribs on furniture, or trip myself up on the rug. I put my back into the doorframe, popped through, and levelled the gun by instinct.

A long and lovely pair of cream-colored legs greeted me, rising all the way up from the floor to the hem of a well-worn UC Santa Cruz t-shirt. Plenty of women have woken up next to me wearing one of my t-shirts, but none of them filled it out like this.

I dropped the gun to my side and it knocked against the moulding.

"Well, good morning." She turned from the stove with a playful smile and the devil in her eyes.

"Morning!" I blurted, panicking to lose the piece. I backed out into the living room and gently placed the gun on the bookshelf. "I see you found my record collection."

"I like to have it on when I cook... music, I mean."

"Did it have to be Sinatra? I thought maybe some more unsavory visitors had shown up."

"Sorry." She laughed and leaned back from the stove to apologize. "First thing I found. I like Sinatra, met him once when I was a little girl. He gave me a Malibu Barbie for my sixth birthday. I had no idea who he was."

Sinatra stories were wearing thin for me—seems like everybody had one lately. Maybe it was me, and I just had The Chairman on the brain.

I shuffled into the kitchen behind her, eyes drifting helplessly to the tight hula going on under my t-shirt as she whisked eggs in a bowl.

"I had eggs?" My eyes remained glued to the top of her long legs.

"Hope you don't mind." She smiled. "I was just going to come wake you up. I assumed you'd be hungry. How are you feeling?"

"Like a seven-foot-tall Nazi with a two-by-four just pummelled me."

I couldn't remember what, if anything, had happened through the long black night. Usually if a woman was wearing my t-shirt in the morning, it was because we were both too drunk to know where I'd pulled her clothes off the night before. I made my way to the small kitchen table and sat gingerly against the wall, desperate for coffee— still hadn't had one since the Hi-Lo, and my body was crawling with need. For a guy with an addictive personality, who usually drinks a couple of pots a day and not much else, going that long without is tantamount to going through heroin withdrawal.

I struggled out of the chair to make myself a hot one, but barely slid my ass off the chair before the steamer on the cappuccino maker kicked in. I sat back down unsure of exactly what was happening, wondering if I was still asleep, or dead from Bradley's bad pills. Soft hands set a perfectly coiffed, king-sized cappuccino in front of me, leaving me speechless. If she was sexy before, now she was pure Roman goddess. I immediately had the urge to tear that shirt right off her and do really bad things on my own kitchen table, despite the lingering pain in every cell of my body.

She obviously saw the expression of awe on my face.

"I worked as a barista while in college," she said, mock-humble. "Before Starbucks ruled the world and every other hipster started calling a latte a macchiato."

"Marry me." That was a joke—mostly.

She play-slapped me like a waitress in a truck stop, and went about her business.

I took a sip of the coffee, and it was a liquid dream—perfect espresso and soft, cloud-soft, velvet layer of steamed magic. My focus shifted to her legs again as she flipped eggs and mixed hashbrowns in a skillet. Was there any portion of this woman that was not perfect? How could she possibly be from the same gene pool as that ugly old bastard, Obie Stetch?

"So, if you stayed *here* last night.... What about Holly?"

"It's the third weekend of the month. Time for Holly's dad to pretend he cares, for a whole 48 hours out of the month."

The bitterness was almost solid in her mouth. I could picture it between her teeth.

"Who is he?" I asked, more competitive than curious.

"Anthony Price. He's a shit. A shit like my father is a shit. A music manager shit with a skeezy chin-beard and a Bluetooth glued to his ear."

She stabbed at the eggs with the spatula. My frying pan had never been happier that I'd bought silicone.

"I guess you know what they say, about girls being attracted to men like Daddy?" She shook her head, still mutilating the eggs.

"Well, at least he's willing to spend some small amount of time with Holly, right? You wouldn't believe how many of my cases are deadbeat dads who run out on their families and leave their kids high and dry. Nothing pisses me off more than people hurting kids."

"I hate that Holly has to be one of those kids. I was one of those kids." Her voice and expression changed, now less angry than sad.

I wanted to hold her. It didn't help that I'd been a prick the night before, implicating her father in crimes she knew nothing about.

"I was too," I said. "That's why it pisses me off. Sorry about what I said about your father last night. I was angry after getting my ass handed to me, and in pain, and being awful to you. Sorry."

She stood stiff and wordless for what seemed like an eternity.

I, in turn, sat uneasy, quietly berating myself, the only sound in the room the slapping of the spatula against the pan. The longer the silence lingered, the more positive I became that I'd blown it.

By the time she spoke again, I was ready to throw myself out of my own kitchen window.

"I know what kind of a bastard he is," she said flatly. "You asked about my mother last night? I don't even remember my mother. I was raised by nannies and babysitters. Most of them quit when he got grabby with them, some when he wouldn't pay up, even after he probably attacked them. He's never hurt me, *physically* or anything, but he's never been much of a father either. He's just the only thing I know. After thirty-five years, he's the only thing that's always been around. But I don't want Holly to go through that. That's why I divorced Anthony. She deserves better. I deserved better.'

We had an awkward minute or two of silence. I sipped on my coffee, and she finished what had, by way of unleashed fury, gone from bacon and eggs to a pan scramble. She set the plate in front of me and sat down to poke at her food with a fork.

I set straight to devouring mine, as much to have something to distract me from the situation as to fill my aching gut. After a few seconds of watching me shovel it in, she set down her fork and put her hand across the table on top of mine. I looked up into softer eyes than I could have hoped to expect.

"Why were you *one of those kids*?" Her voice was tender and tinged with sadness.

I stopped eating and slurped some coffee to clear my mouth of debris. A tremendous amount of warmth exuded from this woman, the same woman I'd wanted to ravage mere minutes before. I never talked about myself with women. Shit, I hardly talked about myself with *anyone* anymore, but something in those eyes made me more comfortable than I'd been in years. I wanted to tell her everything, every minute of my life, every lousy miserable secret that was currently jockeying to choke my windpipe. More than anything, I feared scaring her off. Still, I didn't seem to have a choice in the matter. My brain was betraying me and my voice was already loading the cash in the getaway car.

"My folks died when I was ten. I don't remember them much, just scattered moments and little images, snapshots of different moments together. My mom, she was gorgeous, like Sophia Loren—dark and lovely and exotic. Very Italian, just like Pops. My dad, he was a pilot. His parents were Irish, passed down the pale skin and strawberry-blonde hair. From what I remember, they were good people and loved me as much as anybody could love a kid. I don't remember a single bad day with them. I remember they were always touching each other, always holding hands and kissing.

"One day they went for a day trip out to the islands in his little DeHaviland Twin Otter. It was their anniversary, time for a little picnic out on Santa Nicolas. A storm hit on their way back, nothing major, but another flier—less experienced, freaking out and not listening to air traffic—flew right through them. They were halfway to the mainland.

"When they found them, they figured my Dad died instantly, but my mom... well... she was in the water, hopefully unconscious, when the sharks got to her."

Rose sat mortified, hand over her mouth in disbelief, tears streaming from her eyes. Her hand closed tight on mine as she shook her head. "My God. I'm so, so sorry. That's terrible."

I smiled weakly. "My grandfather was the only other family I had, and he was out of the country at the time. It took three years for him to find out what had happened and come back for me. In the meantime, I got bounced from home to home, past some real lousy excuses for human beings—people who took kids like me for the government checks, then treated us worse than their house pets."

Something wet slid down my cheek, and I wiped it away with my forearm and laughed nervously.

"I had no idea...."

I laughed off another wet smear and smiled. "When Pops came back, though, everything changed. He took care of me, took me crazy places and showed me the world. It was a cool way to grow up, all over the world." I feigned a cough and turned away to wipe my eyes.

"Would you like another cup?" she asked, motherly smile standing on those lips.

"Huh, yeah." I choked. "That was the best damn coffee I've had in years."

She nodded with a soft look in her eyes and stood to take the cup.

I took her hand and smiled up at her. "Thank you, Rosie." I tried to impart all my feelings for her through the color in my eyes.

She touched my face gently with her other hand, then bent down and kissed me softly on the lips. A lightning bolt of giddy pleasure and joy shot up from my knees and into my chest, as if a rocket had just gone off inside of me.

She took the cup and went to the coffeemaker, and began to bang out the grounds and set up to make another cup.

I'd never felt that way about a woman before. I did okay with the ladies, especially the ladies in the places I frequented—sad-eyed wilting flowers, lonely and betrayed housewives, and drunks past their prime. This felt different.

It was a combination of that fluid rush I got in ninth grade, getting a smile and a note from Betsy Kornblum in homeroom; and the crazy, adrenalized passion that filled my muscles and burned like lava the first time I took Eva Priest for a ride, full of Kentucky bourbon and a couple of lines of coke.

Some kind of frustrated ecstasy overwhelmed me, driving a need to pull this woman right into my soul. I couldn't stand it anymore. She was driving me crazy.

I went to her and pressed myself tight against her back. The ripe curve of her supple ass pressed against me, and I put my hand around her stomach, feeling the solidness of her body through the t-shirt. My lips went to her neck and her ears, all of her tasting as sweet as I'd imagined. I spun her around fast and hard, and pulled her into me, mashing our lips together hard enough to feel teeth. Her heartbeat thumped through those lips, and I wanted to devour them whole.

She moaned softly once, and her hands found the waist of my pants and tore down. Then she backed against the counter and flicked her tongue into my mouth. We hit the floor and rolled.

Sinatra was still serenading from the other room.

Chapter 10

When we finally came up for air, it was mid-afternoon and we lay beside the bed, wrapped in sheets damp with sweat. Most of my aches and pains had been forgotten. My shoulder still screamed like a rotten bastard, but a little of the mobility had returned.

I got up and went to the kitchen, and made us a couple of drinks—Mrs. Bradley's bathtub scotch for her, ice water for me. When I came back, she was snuggled up in the bed under the down comforter, looking as gorgeous as the first moment I'd seen her. I flipped a pillow up against the wrought iron head-frame and sat next to her, holding the drinks.

"Wow! You really brought the A-game there."

"Thanks?"

"Mrs. Bradley was right. You are trouble, Mossimo Cole."

"Jesus! Let's not talk about *her* right now." I laughed.

I set the drinks down on the side table and leaned over her for a long, luscious kiss. Then I leaned back against the pillow and retrieved her drink.

"I thought you didn't drink?"

"I don't. Shouldn't. Mine's water. This is for you."

She took the glass and sniffed at it before taking a sip. "Holy shit! What is that?"

"I think it's supposed to be scotch."

A long silence passed between us as she nuzzled into the crook of my arm, and we just lay next to each other. I was glad she hadn't asked more about the booze. I didn't want to talk about that. Not with her. Not yet. I was feeling good, and in control of myself for the first time in a long time.

She held her head up off my chest, tracing pictures and making trails with her fingers, and I waited for the inevitable questions. Would they be about the tattoos first, or the scars?

"What are these from?" She poked a series of gnarled circles that ran across my chest.

Scars first. You can tell a lot about the woman by what she's curious about. The ones that really care go for the scars. The disposable fun-time girls always ask about the ink. Either way, I had nothing to hide. I just wish she hadn't picked those ones first.

"Cigarettes," I offered, matter-of-factly. "A coke dealer by the name of Jimmy Two-Four thought I was screwing his wife...."

"Were you?"

"A little," I replied, smirking. "I didn't know she was *his* wife."

"And this?" She fingered a raised crater in the middle of a Celtic knot design on the front of my left shoulder.

"Cheating wife who lost a five-million-dollar settlement because of some pictures I took."

"And this one?" A thick purplish line across the middle of my right deltoid muscle, like it was underlining the 'SPQR' that was inked right above it in dark Roman lettering.

"Machete. Missing person, runaway kid who turned out to be an ice-head gangbanger not too keen on going home to his cornholing Baptist Minister father."

"Jesus, look at you! What about this?" She poked at a wide pink scar snaking from just below my ribs up to the middle of my chest.

"I got shot. Part of the reason I don't drink."

She glared at me and turned her head slightly, begging the question.

"I was trailing this politician, followed him to a bar, ended up getting soused. I lost control of the situation and ended up shot by his security detail, in the liver and kidney, of course. Two big reasons I don't drink anymore. I guess I'm not that great at my job."

She sat up with a frown and looked me over, seemingly for the first time, taking in the whole picture. The whole mural, really — a roadmap of misery and misadventure. Her scrutinizing eyeballs settled exactly where I knew they would, on the mangled calf of my right leg, partially obscured with a large and intricate Polynesian tribal pattern.

"And do I even have to ask how this happened?"

"Vendetta."

She ran her hands over the snaking scar and missing chunk of muscle. The look on her face made it clear that I wouldn't get away with such a trite response, so I made with the brutal truth and hoped she'd still respect me in the morning, so to speak.

"I was seventeen, romantic about death and vengeance — especially about the death of my parents. I was going to kill every goddamn shark I could find off the coast of Santa Nicolas."

"And did you?" Incredulity dripped from the words as they hung in the air. She had that way that only a mother has, of immediately pointing out your stupidity without ever hinting at the word itself.

"A couple."

"Then what?"

"Then this." I nodded towards my leg. "It was the first time we'd been back to California. I was all kinds of messed up. I'd go out in this little cutter I borrowed from one of Pop's old fishing buddies, get ripped out of my tree, then start dumping chum in the water and wait for the nasty fuckers to show up. Then I'd just blast the shit out of the water with a hunting rifle.

"One night, a little more drunk than usual, the recoil caught me off guard. I tripped, or slipped—however it happened, I ended up in the water with a handful of them. Luckily, even drunk, confused and panicking, I'd studied them so long and thought about it so much, it was almost second nature to know where to stick the knife. I got one of them, put the knife in his gills, and was so blinded by rage and booze and adrenaline, I didn't even feel it when he grabbed onto my leg.

"When the others came running, and the clouds of red surrounded me, my senses returned to me. I twisted the knife and practically buried my hand up to my elbow in the side of that ugly bastard. He opened up his trap, and I doubt anybody has ever shot up out of the water so fast. Thank Christ I was right next to the ladder, or they probably would have finished the snack. I'm guessing the rest of them set on the one I'd carved up, because I remember the water boiling up with red fury as I dragged myself onto the deck and scrambled for the first aid kit.

"I somehow managed to tie off my leg and turn the boat around, and bring it in before I passed out. I radioed in and an ambulance was waiting. I just told them I'd fallen overboard and torn my leg open. Pops was not happy. He knew. I could tell he knew, the second he walked into that hospital room and glared at me."

"Jesus. What did he say?"

"He didn't *say* anything. He sat down and shook his head. He came back every day and just sat there, talking baseball and bringing me old pulp detective novels to read. He didn't say anything about it until the day I walked out of the hospital on crutches."

Rosie lay rapt with attention. I almost forgot I was telling a story, but she gave me a painful nudge in the side and raised her lovely eyebrows to urge me on.

"We got in the car, which he'd already packed. We were going away again. He just said, 'Sorry, kid, guess you weren't ready.' That was that. He never mentioned it again. We just kept on running around the world, having our little adventures. It was a weird way to live, like bandits half the time, begging for rides, sneaking across borders, sleeping on floors."

"Sounds... interesting," she said, still running her hands over me, walking her fingers over my muscles, and what used to be muscles.

"I know how it probably sounds, like he was irresponsible or something, but it was wild, like being the kid in a Spielberg movie. If I said I wanted to learn about pyramids, we were in Cairo by the end of the week. He always knew someone who would take us in, like family. The whole world was our family."

"You just bummed around? You didn't go to school or anything? What about high school?"

"Never went. I did correspondence courses sometimes, passed all of the tests, and knew enough to get into UCSC, then the Police Academy. It was cool, though. I had a great life with Pops. We were more friends than anything. That's how he was. We spent my sixteenth birthday on a luxury liner going from Turkey to France. I lost my virginity to a thirty-seven-year-old Viennese heiress. She rode me like a prize stallion night after night. The only thing Pops had to say, one morning when I came down for breakfast with a big smile on my face... he said, 'A gentleman would have washed the pussy off his fingers before he reached for the juice.'"

She did not seem as amused by that as I was.

"Gross." She sat up and sipped at her drink. "So you just bummed around the world, partying it up with your ol' grandpa, getting beat up, getting laid, getting drunk...."

A little venom laced her voice, a touch of.... What? Resentment? Jealousy?

"No, there was hardly any of that. In fact, Pops hated that I drank. It was always a problem between us. I promised to quit, and after I got shot, he got sick. You don't squelch on a deathbed promise to an Italian grandfather."

She laughed at that.

"You sound like that guy who called asking about Dad's record."

The air in the room suddenly made itself scarce. "What guy?"

"Testaverde? He said he worked for a record collector who might be interested in buying the record if it turned up."

"Let me guess," I growled. "*Joseph* Testaverde."

"Yeah, do you know him? He was very nice over the phone. He sounded charming and polite."

She meant it to be a flirtatious joke, to see if she could get a rise out of me. She'd even accompanied it with a sly wink.

I didn't bite. "Joey Thumbs. His name is Joey Thumbs. They call him that on account of how he likes to torture people by breaking the bones in their hands, starting with the thumbs. Stay away from him."

"I suppose you're going to tell me he's some kind of scary gangster, right?"

"He is."

She laughed again, a hearty, self-assured laugh. She no doubt meant it to prove how little she was frightened, how she could take care of herself.

"I'm serious. You and Holly need to stay away from that psycho. Who do you think arranged this?" I stood and pulled my shorts on, letting her drink in the full extent of my purple, bruised and battered self. "I know you think this is all ridiculous, grown men getting violent over a bloody record, but this is a very bad man, worse than anything you might have dealt with before. He's a killer."

She raised her hands in mock supplication, then downed the rest of her drink. "Okay, Cole, I will stay away from the mafia."

She still thought it was a joke.

"Rosie—"

She put her hand up to my face and shook her head. "My father is Obie Stetch. I've been surrounded by drug dealers and gangsters and gang-bangers and thugs since the day I was born."

There was obviously no sense in pursuing it, so I shrugged and lay back down beside her.

"You're a big girl," I said.

She hugged the comforter to her chest and turned her head away.

I felt the relationship souring even before it began. What was I doing wrong? No clue, but I didn't want to do it again—didn't want to walk away from another woman who might be *the* woman.

"I'm sorry, Rose." I laid my hand on top of her delicate, pale fingers.

She smiled, wrapped her fingers between mine, and shuffled back down to lay beside me. "Tell me more about Pops." She nuzzled into my neck.

"He had cancer, all through him by the end. They gave him six months, and he fought it for ten."

The words fell out of me without so much as a consultation with my brain. My chest ached at the thought of it, but my mouth couldn't stop moving.

"When he was finally at the end, he told me he didn't want to die that way, already buried in sheets and tubes and machines. He made me promise to always say that the end had come more valiantly. He wanted the world to hear that we had been out, climbing through slick caverns and over a dangerous precipice or two, before he lost his footing and fell, swallowed up in the fog and the mist of a great waterfall, lost like Sherlock-fucking-Holmes. He loved Sherlock Holmes. That was Pops. That was his story, what he always told me. 'Don't settle for just being a man. Always be the hero.'"

"Jesus. That's a mind fuck and a half."

I'd never told anyone that before. It was the last thing he said to me before he died. He stared me in the eyes and held my arm so hard he nearly broke it. He heard me promise, and then he was gone... and I was alone. Finally, utterly and completely alone. The same feeling simultaneously welled up in my chest and pushed me down by the shoulders.

"Makes me wonder how much of the rest of it was bullshit," I said, trying to laugh it off.

"You really loved him, didn't you?" She still stared at the picture, doing it, at least in part, to spare me the embarrassment of her seeing me tear up. She also seemed to be examining every detail of that lost moment, looking for a clue or an indication of what she'd gotten herself into.

"I loved my grandfather more than anything in this whole world. I didn't really have a choice about it. He's all I had."

She looked up at me, teary-eyed and exuding a warmth of understanding. "Well, that's how I feel about my father too. I can't avoid it. I've got nothing else to hold on to."

I lay back and set my head on the pillow, staring at the ceiling in uncharacteristically deep thought.

"No... you have everything. You have Holly, and now you get to try to turn her into a perfect you."

I had no idea where that came from. I usually tried to keep the profound thoughts from passing anywhere near my voice box. Whether it was what I said, or how I said it, an uncomfortable, loaded silence filled the room, until only the barely audible hiss of the speakers in the next room remained, as the record player waited for its next meal.

I gave in first, and rolled to stare intently into those deep emerald pools of hers. "I'm sorry. I mean, I don't know you or your daughter. I should just keep my damn-fool mouth shut for once and—"

"That's not how it's supposed to work. I don't want her to be *me*. I want her to learn from my mistakes and be better than I am."

"Like I said, I usually have no fucking idea what I'm talking about."

She rolled up onto her knees beside me, and took my face in one slender hand and kissed me. "You think too much, Cole, but I like you. You're sweet."

With one clumsy, child-like move, she flopped back down in bed next to me and laid her head on my chest. "Most guys I end up with, they're the kind of guys that spend my money, move into my house.... They always end up needing rides everywhere, and I end up a glorified assistant who takes it on the couch."

"That is a terrible euphemism. *Take it on the couch*?"

She playfully slapped my chest and nudged me in the ribs with a fist, which almost set me to screaming with pain. When she started kissing my neck, all pain and common sense left my body, which must have been exactly the effect she was looking for.

The phone rang, and I let the machine get it. We lay there necking like horny teenagers while a decidedly Japanese accent left a proper message regarding an urgent matter of great import—probably a telemarketer, trying to sell me something. I didn't need any coupons to the local Sushi house. I was busy. Very busy.

"So how do you want to spend your Saturday night, Cole?" Her lips worked their way down my non-bruised side.

I sat bolt upright and looked for the clock on the side table. 5PM.

I fell out of the bed and scrambled to grab my clothes and ran out the door toward the bathroom. "*Fuck!*"

"*Hey! What the hell?*" she yelled after me.

"Sorry, I have to be somewhere tonight. I need a shower and I'm already running late." I grimaced and yelled from the bathroom, "Do you think you could give me a ride?"

I could only imagine the look on her face.

Chapter 11

She dropped me off outside of Dingo's at six. She declined my offer for her to stay and have a drink and watch the show, saying she wanted to go home and get cleaned up. Oddly disappointing, as I wanted to show her off to Danny, and really, probably could have used her help to avoid getting entangled in his usual madness. Instead, we made plans for dinner the next night—me, Rosie, and Holly. Serious business.

I'd never dated a mom, never really had to deal with a kid in my adult life, and couldn't even remember the last time I'd met a client's kid—any kid. To say my nerves were on edge about the whole thing would be the understatement of a lifetime, but I tried to play it cool, promising to see what else I could find out about the record, and she promised to ask her father about Mary.

As I opened the door, she grasped my hand and held me back, diving over the console and kissing me—a long, slow, passionate kiss that said I should call her after playing with my friends. I stepped out of the car and retrieved my bass from the back seat, which proved handy in hiding the massive erection currently pointing to magnetic north.

I waved goodbye as she drove off, then turned to find Foxy Thunders, *Rock Star*, in skin-tight black jeans and a baggy black t-shirt floating over his pasty-white, petite frame. He flicked his trusty Irish dagger into the frame of a door, ten feet away from him, and ambled to pick it out of the wood, then returned to his spot to repeat his fun.

I shouted from the parking lot, "What happens if somebody comes out that door, asshole?"

"Guess they'd be fucked, mate." He smirked. "That was some kind of special g'bye ye just got there, *Moss-ee-moe* Cole."

He flicked the knife again, a glint of steel in the light before the resounding *thwock* of it burying itself in the already mangled door. Foxy Thunders—still just Danny Fox to his mother and his oldest pal—had been playing this game as long as I'd known him. He'd lost that knife a hundred times, but somehow, he always got it back—from cops, bouncers, airport security. Mrs. Bailey had taken it away every time he set foot in the neighborhood. He was seventeen the first time she said,

"Last thing I need is a drunken mick with a knife, messing up my mouldings."

Danny vaulted over the railing of the stairs and landed at my feet, stealthy as a damned jungle cat. "Think yer fire-haired maiden'd kiss *me* like that, Mossy?"

"She wouldn't touch you with your own fingers. Mrs. Bradley says hello, by the way. Next time just call me on the telephone."

"Yeah, she chased the limo halfway down the block, swinging fer the fences with that goddamn broom of hers." He giggled like a kid that just lifted a ten-cent candy. "So which one kicked yer arse, then? Ol' Boozy Bradley? Or your high-quality ginger lass there?" He threw a few light jabs at my midsection and fluttered around me like some kind of monochrome ghost.

I swatted him down with a left and threw a foot into his ass, knocking him in the gravel, just like when we were kids.

"I should have stayed home," I grumbled. "It would have spared me looking at you in those ridiculous pants."

"Well, let's talk about that. What, exactly, is wrong with me pants? Ye wish ye could wear pants this sexy, ye fat old twat."

"Arse!" I hugged him, a slight brogue slipping into my voice as it always did around my oldest, dearest and most insufferable friend.

"I tease, but y'know it does my heart good to see ye, brother." He kissed me on the cheek. "So who did fuck up yer ugly face then? Ye look like absolute shite, Mossy."

Danny Fox was not just my very best friend; he was frequently my only friend. This despite the fact that he looked like a teenage douchebag, and had the foul-mouthed Irish charm of a septuagenarian Dublin dockworker. He was something of a celebrity these days, face all over MTV and body spray commercials. Foxy Thunders, last of the old-school punk rockers, though the kids seemed to think of him as a brand new phenom. He had a few hits: *Spankin' The Balzac*, *Oi Honkey*, *Gorilla Ballz* and, of course, the ubiquitous *Cleveland Steamer*.

I sat in on bass with his band, The Atomic Sphinkters, on occasion, more as a chance to spend time with Danny and sweat out some aggravation than any pretence of fame or fortune. He insisted, really, and never let up about making me join his traveling circus on a regular basis. He was five-and-a-half feet and ninety-eight pounds of the most aggravating, free-willed, and totally batshit insane person I'd ever known.

Ninety minutes later, we worked through the final sound check, and I nursed a cup of mellow Kona goodness. Danny always made sure they had the best coffee on brew, if I was going to be playing with the band. He tore through life like hell on two legs, ninety-nine percent of the time, but if you called him friend, he was your *best* friend.

I was still riding a decent high from my day with Rosie and the percs I downed before leaving. Mixed with the fine coffee coursing through my veins, it made this a pretty good evening, despite the lingering pain and incessant throb in my face, ribs, shoulder and hands. I had a little bit of trouble at first, getting the bass in a comfortable position, working my fingers loose on the strings and stretching them out to hit the notes properly. Five minutes oiled me up enough to play most of Danny's tunes, and I only lagged a little on Black Flag's *T.V. Party* and Fishbone's *If I was in Charge.*

Danny had been doing the same straightforward set list for years, and the rest of the band was thrashed, so no worries for me. Just a nice relaxing night of hammering the strings, sweating off a couple pounds, and maybe drinking a careful few beers. I finally felt whole, more like myself.

We made our way out the back of the club, toward a Chicken & Waffle place a block over, hoping to avoid any fans camping out for a look at His Majesty, Foxy Thunders. We were shit out of luck, as a throng of shapely young women in all manner of ripped-up black t-shirts, leather and latex converged on us. There was more black eyeliner and lipstick on display than at a Hot Topic outlet store. Danny surveyed the crowd, jumped onto the guardrail in front of us, and leapt a good ten feet to the top of his limo.

It never ceased to amaze me how effortless his shenanigans always seemed. If I'd tried that, I would have busted out my teeth and looked like an old moron.

Danny stood defiantly, looming over the crowd, and with his best Shakespearean flourish, announced himself as loud as could be. "Good evenin', ladies! I bid ye all adieu! I'm off to eat waffles and bed virgins with me very best mate. Be sure to catch the show, and maybe we'll see some of ye lovely young things for a little bed and breakfast come the impassioned strains of the Sun's early rising!"

I shook my head and shoved my way through the crowd, elbowing a three-hundred-pound beast of a girl in combat boots and a pink tutu out from in front of the car door, planted my ass in the back seat, and hauled Danny in through the sunroof. The sea of young sex parted in front of the car and, despite them chasing us half a block, we were soon free of flailing limbs and hands slapping against the car like the Devils mambo.

It was mildly disconcerting trying to explain my story to Danny as he blew kisses at the mass of white-faced, black-haired vixens swooning outside the window, but by the time our entrees were on the table, I'd laid out the basics.

"So now ye've got the mafia, the sex fiends, Lord knows who else, and Obie fuckin' Stetch breathin' down yer neck over a Sinatra record? Better be a fuckin' good one! I mean, that's what these hard cunts are all up in tight over? A fuckin' Sinatra record? I love ol' Frankie as much as the next guy—more, probably. Y'know I love the early stuff."

I took a bite of my sweet potato pie and a swig of coffee, looked around to make sure no one was listening, then leaned in to tell Danny my secret. He bent forward conspiratorially, laughing as he did.

"Frank and Ella Fitzgerald, 1948 at the Mozambique Club. The only time they were recorded together other than on TV." I whispered as if giving up Nixon at the Watergate.

He sat back, befuddled, either by what I had just told him, or by the six ounces of whiskey he'd consumed from his hip flask since we'd sat down.

"Fuckin' hell, Mossy. That there is the holy fuckin' grail of American jazz recording. I mean, Ol' Blue Eyes was strugglin' at the time, but singin' with Miss Ella? Back then? Bloody fuckin' brilliant!"

He paused for a second, stroked his chin as he frequently did, and then shot back forward, another of his odd twitches.

"They offered ye fifty grand, and beat yer face to pudding fer that? Somethin' ye didn't even have to give em'?"

"Well, to be fair, the gay porn stars did that before the 'Black Hand' even showed up. Thought they were showing initiative, I guess."

He snickered and popped back against the booth, and stretched his arms out to both sides, as if he was about to wrap them around a couple of fair maidens. "You need to see the Swede, boyo. I think this record of yers would be worth a helluva lot more than fifty G. The Swede, he'd know."

"The Swede?" I downed another slug of coffee.

"Aye. He specializes in the finding of very rare recordings, especially when there's underhanded or possibly semi-legal and otherwise questionable acquisitions to be made. Best on the west coast. Ye need a record? He'll be the man to see."

I dabbed at the crumbs left on my plate, and waved at the waitress for a refill on my joe. "All right then, where and when?"

"Well, what fuckin' time is it, anyways?"

I dug my watch out of my pocket and gazed through increasingly bleary eyes. "It's almost nine, Danny." My voice dripped with no small measure of irritation. "We need to get back to the gig."

"All right, all right." He threw up his hands up to ward off my pissy tone. "Let me get the bill. They aren't likely gonna start the show without the main attraction now, are they? We'll go see The Swede tomorrow mornin'. Pick me up at noon."

I sipped at my coffee, then lay my head back against the booth seat, nudging my hat down over my eyes. "Noon is not part of what most people consider the morning, Danny."

"What do ye know, Mister Fancy P.I.? With yer fancy fuckin' hats and yer fuckin' pocket watch... you look like *my* goddamn grandfather half the time. We need to get ye out with some young chickies, get ye laid more than once a decade, ye sad, sad excuse fer a man."

"Fuck you, *Foxy Thunders*. You're thirty-five and dressed like Bono's little sister." I laughed from under my hat.

"You wanker! Bono's what now? I'll fuck ye dead! Fuckin' Bono! That's a low blow there."

"And nobody says 'chickies', you twat."

"Fuck you," he barked. "American cunt!"

I peeked out from under my hat to catch him trying to lean over the table and pour sugar into the brim of my hat. The waitress caught him too, as she stepped up to the table and filled my cup, and gave Danny a filthy look of reprisal.

"I hope you're gonna clean up that mess!" She grumbled and slapped our bill on the table in no uncertain terms.

"Sorry, darlin'," Danny mumbled. "Just havin' a little fun. I'll sweep it up and make sure he takes it with him."

He smiled his charming, boyish, emerald rogue smile, and the annoyance melted from her face.

"Well, just don't leave a mess, all right?"

Showtime was imminent at ten. Danny and the boys had polished off the better part of two cases of beer backstage while the audience flooded into the club and crowded the three small bars. I peeked out from behind the thick old velvet curtain to survey the crowd of unwashed, too-cool twenty-somethings and blazed-out thirty-year-olds. A decent-sized crowd for Dingo's, maybe 200 people smoked, drank, and yammered away over the yowling cacophony of the opening band, a bunch of greasy kids in skinny jeans and Flock of Seagulls hair, wailing out watery covers of Sex Pistols and System of a

Down.

They finished and shambled backstage to put on their nonchalant faces and let us know how unimpressed they were by the punk legend and his band of old men. Danny laughed and kissed their singer on the mouth as the P.A. began to blast a barely-recognizable and totally garbled Stooges tune. The kid looked like he was going to shit his pants—probably did, not that anybody would notice.

Danny gave his usual "Once more unto the breech" spiel and slapped each of the band members on the ass. I gave him a small shot to the arm as he ran past and stepped back into the shadows of the speaker stacks. We took the stage a minute later, the guitar player, drummer and I stumbling out in the dark and groping for our weapons, while the almighty Foxy Thunders, God of Punk Rock, walked to the middle of the stage, turned his back to the crowd, and waited for the spotlight to hit.

When it did, we all plowed into the Dead Kennedy's *Too Drunk To Fuck*, the go-to standby for an L.A. show. Danny played the crowd, stomping around the stage, pouring a beer over his head, and tossing fingers off at the audience as he screamed into the microphone.

We segued into *Cleveland Steamer*, pulling it like taffy into a seventeen-minute dervish of noise and attitude. Danny followed that with an introduction of the band, the usual shmoozy-shmaltz where he talked me up as his half *eye-talian* brother and extolled my virtues as a multi-instrumentalist and musical virtuoso, all of which likely bored the shit out of these hipsters and rage-filled, post-teen punkers.

So I took matters into my own hands and thumped out the bass line for the ultimate classic, MC5's *Kick Out The Jams*, which always landed Danny—hook, line and sinker. He stomped back to center stage shooting his fist into the air screaming, "KICK OUT THE JAAAAAAAMS, MOTHER FOOOOOOOKEEEEERS!" in his thick brogue. We butchered a steady stream of classics—*Sonic Reducer, Clampdown,* even *Jet Boy* by the New York Dolls.

I always loved the Dolls.

About halfway through the show, and halfway through *Gorilla Ballz,* I saw them: Kickerdick and Manlove, in the flesh. Manlove showed first, completely inconspicuous in jeans and a black t-shirt. I almost wouldn't have been able to place him without that telltale shiner, compliments of yours truly. It took me a little longer to find the big ink monkey, in the middle of the mosh pit at the front of the stage, tossing wannabes around like ragdolls. Kickerdick was obviously in his element and enjoying every minute of it. He must have been a masochist, smashing himself around in that vortex of flesh and bone with the injuries he must have been nursing.

I couldn't have done it in my battered state.

The real question was whether it was coincidence, the cruel humors of fate, the ten-cent buffalo wings, or another pressing appointment with Don DeFrancesco that brought them to Dingo's on a Saturday night.

As long as they weren't bum-rushing the stage or drawing down on me with Lugers or rubber dildos, I'd give the chicken wings the benefit of the doubt and just keep playing.

We finished the first encore, a quick-charging tune called *Helluva Way To Die* from a Canadian band called Wagbeard. Danny and I had seen them play a few times in the mid 90's, and he was thoroughly smitten with the song, which allowed him much opportunity to work his profanity jones.

As I finished my half-bow-half-stagger with the song winding out in a final drum roll, I looked up and locked eyes with Manlove at the bar. He waved to me, a pretty little tea-time wave with the middle two fingers of his right hand, motioning me over to the bar.

I nodded. There were certainly enough people here to keep them from trying to abduct me again, and if anybody could handle the big Nazi, it would be Jimbo, the bouncer—325 pounds and nearly seven feet of prime Lubbock, Texas rawhide. He was the kind of dude you could actually picture eating another person whole, or climbing the Empire State building with Fay Wray in his hand. It always paid to have a friend in Jimbo.

Foxy was busy with groupies and contest winners and fawning agents and hangers-on, so I excused myself to the bar and asked Tony, the drummer, to tell Jimbo to keep an eye on me. I watched for Kickerdick out of the corner of my eye as I made my way through the crowd to Manlove.

"Mr. Menlowe, I presume," I said as he offered me a cold Heineken.

I was so thirsty and so high on the gig, I took a swig, but shoved it just out of reach as I sat on the stool next to him, careful to keep myself turned half-away, to avoid any more ball-smashing incidents.

"I had no idea you were so talented, Mossimo," he said with a lilt.

"So, is this whole suburban gentleman thing...." I laughed, waving my hand to accent my point. "This is the real you? And the tough guy *meshuggenah* is the act?"

"Oh, who's to say, sweetie. We are all of us made up of many men, are we not? I mean, I'm not questioning your fashion sense." He nodded at my chapeau.

I had to give him that one. I also had to holler to hear myself over the crowd and the music. "So did you two come here looking for me?"

He smiled, as sweet-bitchy a smile as I ever saw in my high school years.

"Oh, you flatter yourself, Cole. Nothing so nefarious, I'm afraid. Jurgen loves Foxy Thunders, says he's the reincarnation of Johnny Rotten."

"Johnny Rotten's not dead."

"Oh, I know that, but Yergie likes to say it anyways. He loves the music, so here we are. Helps him get out his aggression, and to deal with the confusion inherent in being a gay masochist jew-lover from Louisiana white trash. Many issues, Mister Cole, but he's really a great big cuddly teddy bear."

"Ahhh." I nodded in complicit understanding. "I'll take your word for that." I pointed towards a lumbering Sasquatch silhouette emerging from the depths of the dance floor. "Here comes your boyfriend now."

Kickerdick skulked towards the bar, an unexpected smile growing on his ugly mug when he saw me. I was even more surprised when he stepped up, wrapped his giant arms around me, and lifted me out of the chair in a bear hug and kissed me.

"Oh man! I feel great! You fucking *rocked*, bro!" he yelled into my face.

I was fairly sure my face was turning blue and, thankfully, he noticed the pained look on my face and dropped me back to my stool.

Then he leaned over and stuck his tongue in Manlove's mouth, which did not particularly help my nausea. Not because they were two men, but because the thought of Kickerdick's tongue in anybody's mouth made me want to cry like sweet baby Jesus.

Once I regained my breath, I felt a little more congenial, especially since they weren't after my spleen or collecting my severed head for Joey Thumbs. Besides, it couldn't hurt to have a couple of bruisers on my team for once. I leaned over to grab my beer and took a long pull—cool and wet, crisp as a three-dollar bill. I let the relief of it wash over me. *Buddha grant me the serenity....*

"Menlowe says you're a big fan," I hollered at the big man, once he'd detached faces with Manlove.

"Fuck yeah!" he bellowed back. "Fucking *Gorilla Ballz* is my song, man!"

I gave him a quizzical look and then stifled the urge to make a joke about *Cleveland Steamer.*

"You wanna meet him?" I asked.

"Are you fucking *serious*?"

I could tell now that Kickerdick was at least six sheets to the wind and loving life—probably a nice mix of pot, ecstasy and German beer. I hauled myself off the stool and waved for them to follow. Jimbo stood stoically blocking the door, until I patted him on a shoulder the size of a side of beef and gestured back at the wonder twins.

"It's okay, Jimbo. They're with me. Foxy said to bring them back."

"I heard I was supposed to watch they didn't kick your fuckin' ass."

"Come on, man, just a couple of ugly fans."

Jimbo moved aside like a drawbridge and eyeballed my guests as they followed. Kickerdick did his best to subvert his natural aggression, but Manlove sidled right up to Jimbo on his way past and gave him a little pat on the ass. Jimbo laid the glare on him, but didn't start any trouble. We carried on into the back, where Danny was ensconced in a sea of partiers and scumbags in expensive suits.

"There he is!" Danny yelled, extracting himself from the mob and taking me by my sore shoulder. "My oldest, dearest friend, Jimmy Cagney's fuckin' Grand-pah!" He laughed.

"Foxy...." I winced, pulling away to the minimum-safe distance. "These are the guys who beat the shit out of me yesterday. Kickerdick and Manlove. Big fans."

Danny looked mildly confused, which quickly morphed into charmingly bemused.

"Holy shite!" He laughed. "Kick-her-dick and goddamn Man-loove. I know you guys. I saw you once at the Balls-Deep, there with a bunch of snooty fashionista-types. Thought it would be a lark to see a 'queer show' and, man, did I love seein' the looks on their faces when ye two started poundin' arse right there on the banquette. How the fuck are ye? Glad to meet ye. Holy shite Mossy! You ever see these two in action? The little fella here did somethin' like the 'dance of seven veils' with a flashlight up his arse! Was fuckin' *magic*!"

Leave it to Danny to be bowled over by the Felix Unger and Oscar Madison of the sex performance world.

As Kickerdick fawned over Danny like a twelve-year-old girl with a Tiger Beat crush, I took Manlove aside to finish our conversation.

"Any news from La Cosa Nostra?"

"I should warn you. That greaseball Testaverde wanted us to bring you in tomorrow. We were supposed to beat the shit out of you again, as a lesson, then bring you back to see him at the same place we took you last time."

"Have you boys turned over a new leaf? You can't abide that kind of violence?"

"Smartass. We just decided we like you a hell of a lot more than we like that Guido nutjob, Joey Thumbs. Besides, he stiffed us on the last job. Still owes us a grand."

"I'm touched. Really."

"A word to the wise, Mossimo Cole. Get your macho little ass out of town. Joey Thumbs doesn't like you, and I was given the distinct impression that he means to finish you off, whether his boss likes it or not."

"Well, thanks for the warning. If you see Joey Thumbs, tell him exactly that. I'm leaving town for a while and have no interest in pursuing any business with him or his boss."

I pulled my money clip out of my pocket and peeled off the couple of fifties they'd just paid me for the show. I handed them to Manlove with my card.

"Here, buy him something pretty." I nodded towards Kickerdick, still rambling in Danny's ear.

"I'm not going to take that. The warning is free, honey. Consider it an apology for messing up your rugged good looks."

"It's not for the info. It's a down payment. I may have some legwork for you boys. Recoup your losses with Joey Thumbs. Call it a retainer."

Manlove stuffed the bills in his pocket and winked at me. "I could live with that. Better than working for those greasy Vegas bastards."

He took my hand and pulled a pen out of his pocket, making quite a show of it all, then scribbled a number on my palm.

"You call us when you need us, Dick."

"You know you could have written that on one of my cards."

"Oh, where's the fun in that?"

I laughed and smiled at him as he winked again and sauntered off to collect the lipstick Nazi, who turned and waved to me as if I were his dear ol' Grandma standing at the door.

I jumped as a hand slapped my ass, sending a lightning bolt of pain up through my back and into my broken ribs.

"Now that's a sweet couple if I ever saw one!" Danny laughed. "Know, I'm thinkin' maybe we should add some Sinatra to the set. I mean, the Pistols did it with *My Way*. McGowan loved Ol' Blue Eyes. Fuck, even Cake does Sinatra. What do you think, Mossy? Maybe somethin' more obscure, like *This Town*, or *Swingin' on a Star*? The big fella thought it was a grand idea."

"Don't be an asshole."

He just smiled at me with his devil's grin and wild eyes. "How's about we get you laid, Mossy boy?"

"Danny...."

Chapter 12

The next hour and a half blurred into a pattern of recurring moments. Danny handed me beers, shoved me toward very young women, talked me up and then disappeared. I protested, relinquished my good sense, drank myself into a bleary-eyed daze, and smiled bashfully at the young girls and their scantily clad bodies. They flashed a lot of flesh, giving me the full dance of the seven veils — not for my sake, but in the hopes that they could leapfrog over me and end up with the main attraction.

By the time the crowd dwindled and Danny finished his goodbyes, I was propped up in a corner, mumbling for courage and wisdom, wedged between a bored label exec rambling off his resume and a pair of nubile young punkers lighting up each other's lady bits. I felt good. I felt numb. Level and completely together for the first time in weeks, maybe months. The sweet, comforting familiarity of a drunken stupor kept me afloat as my head bobbed just above the waves.

Danny scooped me up by an armpit, waved off the exec, and winked at the girl-pretzel as he hauled me to my feet. "Let's go, brother. Always more fun to be had."

Jimbo stepped in front of us and threw an arm out to open the way as we approached the door. Danny paused to slip Jimbo a fistful of bills and a kiss on the cheek. Then we were outside, car parked at the ready, security advisor at the wheel. A small coterie of young ladies with spiked hair and pierced faces screamed and waved as Danny stuffed me into the back of the SUV.

He popped his head out the window as we drove off, blowing them a kiss and declaring his appreciation for their support by hollering, "Next time, I'll fuck every last one o' ye's! And yer mothers!" He fell back into the seat laughing, slapping me on the knee.

My head swam in the sweet, oaty fog of a beer bender.

Danny jumped across the cabin to face me. "Fuckin' hell, that never gets old, does it now? Where the hell are we goin', Moss? Ye want some ladies? Some liquor? Get the ol' knob gobbled?"

"Whatever, man. You're the rock star, I'm just along for the ride.

No girls for me, though. No girls. No sir." I was still flying on adrenaline, Percocet, and the bountiful beers that my organs couldn't process. Orbiting my own stratosphere, there with my best friend, I felt twenty again. It was a feeling I had missed, deeply and desperately.

Every time the little bastard roared into town with his circus and demanded I join up, I secretly wanted to pick him up and scream my undying devotion and everlasting thanks to the heavens. Danny had always known how much these gigs meant to me, how much I wished I could be like him, but he never let on. It was nice when friends lied to each other out of love.

"Billy!" Danny shouted at the driver. "Take us to Eva's! We need some women and some goddamn whiskey, boyo!"

I fell back into my seat, smiling and feeling the calm comfort of my old friends wash over me. "No girls, Danny. No sir. Eva's is lots of girls. No girls allowed."

The booze took complete hold of my brain, replaying my afternoon with Rosie's lips, Rosie's long legs—a swirl of images dancing to a mambo beat.

***

Eva's was a modern-day speakeasy and under-the-radar high-class brothel in Laguna. Eva was a statuesque Southern beauty—one of those women with the velvet accent and the high breeding to own any room she walked into. She had been operating her place for something like twenty-five years, with zero problems—probably due to the fact mayors, millionaires, congressmen, police chiefs and senators all frequented her joint. Rumor had it that a certain former president and a certain action-star-turned-governor had both been big customers through the years.

I'd voted for that president. Couldn't go wrong with a man who played the sax.

Danny dragged me up the wide stone staircase of Eva's estate. My mangled organs were working overtime to filter out the bevy of drinks I'd consumed, and my brain was paying the price. I hated being the cheapest drunk in any room.

Even hammered out of my tree, I had to appreciate the layout: marble and glass and rich wood and leather—as fine as any old Southern mansion in any state. Scarlett O'Hara, eat your heart out.

The boozy sway also failed to numb the sight of a full dozen of the most beautiful women on Earth. Two dozen if you counted with my eyes. Every single one of them was a precise encapsulation of a different archetype of feminine perfection: tall girls, short women, big mamas and petite princesses—all shapes, sizes and flavors. They turned in synch, like a fifty-limbed sex-bomb cephalopod, to greet us with one uniform of wide, sly smiles and smouldering eyes.

I swallowed a hard lump of throat as I struggled through the soup in my brain. *No girls. No sir.* Danny slapped me hard on the back and yelled at the top of his lungs. Or so it seemed. I couldn't really be sure what was real anymore. Case in point—Eva approached in an exquisite slow-motion saunter that rolled like slow tide. The ground gave out beneath me, starting at the knees and ending with the floor holding up my face.

"Why, *Mistah Thundahs*. So splendid to see you again. Been a long time since we've seen you," she purred, then added with a bucket of ice water, "Hello, Cole."

"Hayvva."

"Still having problems with that liver, I see...."

Danny laughed as he hauled me up off the floor and shoved me off to one side, where I found myself in the sturdy arms of a lovely and voluptuous giantess with a Bettie Page haircut and about three feet of very welcoming cleavage.

I excused myself and was rewarded with a squeeze on the ass as I bent over to dust my pants.

She fed me a long, suggestive wink and the tip of her pink tongue swiping slow and suggestive over very red, very luscious lips.

The ol' flagpole begged me for a buff-and-polish.

"You're cute, tough guy," she purred. "Love the ink."

"I'mma jus' go over here for a second."

Danny surveyed the room as a bevy of young, unbelievably attractive women swirled around him like the Sirens from *The Odyssey*. They seemed more entranced by Danny than he was by them. That was the Foxy Thunders magic. Then again, maybe they were really good at their jobs. He chose three girls—tall, blond and lithe like dancers—and wandered away toward the giant spiral staircase in the middle of the room.

The giantess swept me in the direction of the parlor that took up the front of the house.

Danny chased his three girls up the stairs, bounding two at a time with a bellowing laugh that echoed through the entire house. "Here I am, ladies!" he hollered after them. "Your Casanova comes forth like a river!"

He rounded the top of the stairs tripping over his own pants, which were already at his ankles, exposing his talents to anyone unfortunate enough to look up.

I stumbled sideways into a wall and entered the room on my hands and knees, laid out by the strong smell of juniper bushes wafting through the open bay doors.

Eva stretched herself across a chaise close to the grand piano. It was a beautiful thing, all smooth curves and gleaming polish. The piano wasn't too bad either.

"Come on, Moss. You haven't been here in so long. Play me a little somethin'?"

I could never resist this request, no matter how drunk or disorderly I was. I loved that goddamn piano. Eva and I had... *history*, most of it based on the fact I reminded her of a long-lost love back home in Louisiana. She gave me booze and let me play her piano and, sometimes, let me play her.

I'd made myself scarce after I lost my liver and my heart, and just hadn't found my way back here.

Danny was playing "Devil on the Doorstep"—his idea of testing my feelings for Rose Stetch. For a best friend, he sure made a grand nemesis.

I wobbled my way past the gleaming baby grand and parked my ass with a thud in front of the little beat-up bar piano against the wall. It looked about a hundred years old, and tough years at that. Walking into the room, you'd think it was just a kitschy part of the decor, but I knew better. I knew what Eva really wanted, so I cracked my knuckles and tinkled out a little bluesy progression.

"Oh, I have missed you, young man." She grinned from her perch. "Let me buy you a drink, Cole."

"Now, Eva, you know I quit drinking. You don't want to kill me off, do you?" I struggled to clear cobwebs out of the cavernous remains of my head as I worked the keys.

"Doesn't seem like you're stickin' too close to that New Year's resolution, Sugar."

From the corner of my eye, I saw my voluptuous Amazonian admirer enter with a bottle and two glasses, which she set down next to Eva. I knew full well what Eva had in mind, and may have even blushed at my own memories of the many times this game went her way.

She waved off the Amazon pinup, and we were all alone in the big room. It was a wide, lovely room, filled with lovely old things in the best of repair. Plants in art-deco pots lined the walls, and the whole affair was presided over by the warm glow of a magnificent crystal chandelier that could have been straight out of *Gone with the Wind*. Eva played her part very, very well, and was a wealthy and influential woman on account of it. She was also usually lonely and homesick.

I finished tinkling and started picking out the opening notes of *Do You Know What It Means to Miss New Orleans*. I warbled out the song as best as I could manage in my condition, aiming for Dr. John and landing somewhere between Louis Armstrong and Jimmy Durante.

Before the song ended, the pinup had returned with a blessing: a huge, foaming cup of cappuccino, set in front of me on the piano like an offering at the temple of Delta Blues.

I leaned over the cup and breathed in the refreshing heat and strong aroma of hazelnuts and espresso.

"Aww. You remembered." I took a long sip, and the reviving glow of mellow contentment flowed down into my belly. The alcohol seemed to wash right out of me.

"Of course I remember, Moss. I remember everything. You know that. It's just a pity we aren't such good *friends* anymore. One little whiskey wouldn't hurt a soul. We used to have plenty of fun with a few drinks and a few laughs. Who knows what could happen between two bodies like ours," she whispered in that husky, sex- and scotch-soaked growl of hers.

"Oh, I think you know perfectly well what would happen if my body was any closer to yours than it is right now. '*Sides!* We're still friends, honey chile," I warbled to her in my best Southern-fried accent. "We just ain't *cousins* no more."

"That is positively the most dreadful thing you have ever said to me, Mossimo Cole. And your accent is atrocious." She smiled.

Things were getting excessively comfortable again. Eva was the kind of complication that could easily sideline you for a full week before you'd even remember your name. *Fuck me.* The subject needed changing before she got any cozier.

Out of nowhere, everything on my mind tumbled out of me in a torrential downpour. I laid out the whole damnable hot Sinatra story.

Eva groaned, stretching like a cat on her antique divan. "Hmm... I remember Obadiah Stetch. He was a mean, ugly, little man — liked to be rough with the wrong girls and refused to pay for the right ones. He was a bully, that one."

"Yeah, well, that little bully has me all locked up in a neat little box, sinking to the bottom of a deep blue sea."

"Is this record really worth all that?"

"I don't know, darlin'. I don't rightly know." I always took on a trace of that intoxicating accent whenever I was around her.

She rolled like a soft wave against the velvet of the divan, gentle and inviting. "Mmmmm. I love Sinatra, you know. My first time with a man—I was thirteen, I think—Sinatra was playing on the radio. This gentleman, he was one of Daddy's partners, a lovely man, charming and debonair. He bought me my first diamonds."

It was the kind of story that should have been shocking—an older man preying on the young daughter of his business partner. It was the kind of thing they made skinamax flicks about. What was with these men who called themselves fathers? *Jesus.*

"Does that shock you, Mossimo Cole? That I was thirteen when I lost my innocence? I thought you were a man of the world. You and your duchess. I guarantee you, I was more a woman at thirteen than your duchess was at thirty-seven."

"You really don't forget anything, do you?"

"No, I do not, sir. Now how about a real drink and we retire to my quarters, hmm?"

She was more intoxicating than the booze, the music, the girls.

I needed to leave. If I didn't leave fast, I wouldn't be leaving at all. It would be so easy to just fall back in those soft, soothing arms and wallow in velvet for days and days. She would be so good, and so, so bad to me for as long as I wanted.

Eva was sex incarnate. We were so much the same—lonely, sad, broken and horny, seeking so much pleasure to avoid the nasty things in life. I would enjoy every damn minute of it, until she killed me with pleasure—or I got too old or too damaged to care. Something always seemed to be missing when we tried, something that would eventually have me, knowing I'd never get away otherwise, sneaking out the door while she was asleep.

I swallowed down the rest of my cappuccino in a hot blast of pain, and pushed myself away from the piano.

"And where, exactly, do you think you are going, my sweet, sweet boy?" she asked.

I stood and bowed. "I'm afraid I must take my leave, darlin'. Another night, another life, hmm?" It felt empty and cloying and entirely unfair to her.

"Any time, Sugar. I'll be waiting with that whiskey." She managed a slight smile, but it was swallowed-up in the sadness of her lonely eyes.

"I bet you will, Evie. I bet you will." I considered strolling over to kiss her on the forehead, or the cheek, but my consideration didn't end there. It ended with me and Eva in the Japanese soaking tub creating our own tsunami.

Time to go. I nodded and blew her a kiss. Seemed safe enough from ten feet away, but it was still a risky move.

She smiled that sad smile again and winked.

I sighed, hitched my shoulders and walked away. "She was an heiress, by the way, not a duchess."

"I know what she was, you sonofabitch." Even pouting and angry, Eva Priest was a hell of a woman.

I collected my hat from the pinup queen as I entered the foyer, tossed it on my head, and tipped it to the girls still lounging in the hall. "G'night ladies."

I shuffled out the front door. In my mind's eye, Eva, half-submerged in that Japanese tub, was riding me like Sea Biscuit.

Upstairs, Danny's shouts rang out at the top of his lungs: "*Big red shoes! Sweet God Almighty! Big red shoes!*"

I had been unlucky enough, on numerous occasions, to be gifted with the information that this was his safe word when engaged in extracurricular activities. I hesitated for a second, heard him laughing and figured he was probably getting what he deserved.

He'd be pissed to no end that his plan to waylay me with booze and Eva had fallen apart, but he'd forgive me in the morning. He always did, and vice versa.

Eva, I'm afraid, would not be so easy to reconcile.

Intermezzo

To my surprise, my car sat intact at the Hi-Lo when Danny's driver-security guard dropped me off at 5 AM. I slipped the man a fifty, wished him luck with Danny and waved him off.

I got into my car, then after a moment or two of befuddled reflection, realized that I was still too drunk to drive. I popped the trunk, dug out my horn and found the key to the Hi-Lo pocketed inside the case.

It was a blind fumble for the light switch in the dark recess of the kitchen entrance, so I left the lights off in the main room. There was more than enough moonlight pouring down through those "blessed windows of divine inspiration," as Charlie Moses called them. I oiled up the trumpet, then worked a few scales just to warm it up and get used to the mouthpiece with my tender and bruised lips and jaw.

Time for a little Mingus: *Alice's Wonderland*, slow and easy. It wasn't really a trumpet tune, but those are usually the best kind to flow on. Trying to work loose enough to play a sax riff on the horn takes a special kind of focus, exactly what I needed to unravel the tangled strings of thought knotted-up like so many abandoned strands of Christmas lights. Slowly, the hows, the whys, and the wherefores would all fall into place one by one to make a cogent whole.

I started on some Miles Davis: *Odjenar*, I think. As the wail come up out of me and through the muted horn, calm settled over me, and it all laid itself out in my mind.

The Sinatra record was most definitely real. Mary Stetch had commissioned it on the sly for her lover, Jorge Ramone. Good ol' Obie stole the record, probably had the man killed. When Mary found out, she killed herself. Or Stetch gave her a helping hand.

At some point in the 70s, he managed to get laid again and Rosie was the result—Rosie with the red lips, who knew nothing about her own mother. Something didn't sit right with that. The mother thing was a thorn in my corpus callosum. And what happened to Mary Stetch's little girl? The first one, before Rosie?

Poor little Rosie. Sweet Rosie. I shook that turn off and tried to keep on the straight and narrow of the case.

Obie Stetch had a big mouth and an obnoxious sense of self-worth. He'd been bragging since 1948 about his one-of-a-kind record. It was a miracle somebody hadn't killed him for it long ago.

Fast-forward to last week. Somebody lifted it from his room like a discarded paperback. He didn't call the cops — that was the first peculiar thing. He called me instead, probably thinking I'd get it back fast and clean. That pointed to Stetch actually believing it was the mysterious Ramone. That, in turn, pointed the finger at Jorge Ramirez.

Then there were the Vegas boys. Stetch calling in favors? Trying to get it back without paying out? Altogether in character for that lousy prick. The news had gotten to the Big Boss, Tommy DeFrancesco, who wanted it for himself. The mob didn't have it — or any idea where it might be — so it was obviously not out to dealers and fences.

The thief was hiding it, keeping it. They didn't snatch it for sale, or they would have grabbed an armload of shit from that wall and the record would have surfaced. Tommy DeFrancesco would have been spinning it on his Blaupunkt in his mansion on Lake Tahoe. Nope, this was a personal crime. Whoever grabbed the record knew what it was, and they knew they'd have to keep it secret or lose it fast.

Jorge Ramirez was the missing link, and my next step. I'd have to figure out how to track him down after meeting Danny's Swede in the morning. I needed to know what the real stakes were, which meant a value on the record. Nobody was getting killed for a couple grand — not by the mob, anyway. I had a hunch it was going to be a lot more than that. A whole hell of a lot more.

I put down the horn, emptied the spit valve, polished her up, put her back in the case, then locked up the club and went home for some sleep.

Chapter 13

The phone woke me with its impatient rattle and clang. It was Rosie. I'd been dreaming of her lips—her lips and Eva Priest's honeysuckle drawl. What in the hell was wrong with me?

"Good morning. Hope I didn't wake you or *interrupt* anything."

I rubbed the sleep out of my still-swollen eyes and stifled a moan as I absently rolled over onto my bad shoulder. "Hmmm? No. What? No. Just home late—early—you know what I mean."

"Partying late with your friend the rock star?"

"What? No, no. Well, yes." I could feel the guilt dripping off my face and slopping onto the receiver. "I had a couple of beers that somehow turned into a platoon and, next thing I knew—"

"You don't owe me any explanations. We're not going steady *yet,* Archie Andrews. We all need to blow off some steam once in a while."

The memory of those lips caused a lightning bolt of giddiness to shoot up from my queasy stomach and into the back of my very dry throat. I felt like death, run over, dropped flat, and sent headfirst down the mountain. "Yeah, but blowing off steam with Danny is more like sitting on top of a volcano."

"You know what I mean, Cole. I just wanted to call and make sure you were still in one piece."

"I'm fine. Ran into some old pals last night, the Nazi Sasquatch and his little friend, but we're all sorted out now."

"The guys who beat you up?"

"Among others." There was a pause while I waited for the pounding in my chest to give away the whole story. I shook it off as part of a bad hangover. I wasn't going to lie to her, but I didn't have to give her full disclosure either. "I spent most of my night listening to the rock star bullshit twenty-year-old girls."

Another pause, this one coming from the other end. "None for you though?"

I laughed. "Not my speed, honey. I like women, not cheerleaders with painted faces."

"Mmm-hmm. I thought every guy has the cheerleader fantasy. Even Sinatra had his Mia Farrow phase."

"I'm not every guy, sweetheart. These days I go for stunning redhead soccer moms. And enough with the Sinatra already."

Another pause, but this one somehow lighter. "Why do I get the feeling there's something you're omitting there? Are we still on for tonight?'

"That's a pretty hard line of questioning for someone who's not going steady. What time is it? I have to pick up Danny. He's taking me to meet some dude who might know about your father's record." I rummaged on the nightstand for the piece-of-shit excuse for an alarm clock I'd been using. It had been Pops', a seventy-year-old beast that had to be wound, and which rarely kept anywhere close to the right time. It said 7:45.

"It's quarter to eleven."

"Goddammit! I've gotta go. "

"Some dude? No twenty-year-old girls?"

"Now you're just being plain jealous, Betty. Or are you more the Veronica type?"

"Guess you'll just have to wait to find out, Arch."

I blew her a kiss over the phone and told her she was beautiful.

After running through a lukewarm shower, I guzzled down a cold cup of day-old coffee, and threw on some jeans and a Clash T-shirt that was lying in the closet. I grabbed my jacket and a hat and bolted out the door.

Not until I hit the wet grass with my bare feet did I come back for my keys and sunglasses... and my boots.

***

I pulled up in front of the Luxe on Rodeo Drive at exactly 12:04, and had the valet call in a page for Foxy Thunders.

Danny sauntered out the front door about twenty minutes later, accompanied by two nubile young women who were too well dressed, and too surgically enhanced, to be fans—had to be call girls. They parted ways with him at the door, where he hugged them, kissed their hands like a proper Irish gentleman, and then bowed courteously as they entered their cab.

I would have honked and hollered, but I caught sight of a bellboy rushing out to hand him two giant coffee cups, which he accepted with a wink and a palmed twenty dollar bill. I popped the passenger-side door open.

Danny bent down to hand me the cups, rolling his eyes over the top of his designer shades. "Why don'tcha let me get ye a real car, Cole. This piece of shite is fair reprehensible in this kind of neighborhood. I can't be seen drivin' around town with a fella in a Chevy Geo, fuck sakes."

"Shut up and get in the fucking car, Princess."

"What kind of way is that to talk?"

I shook my head and started away from the hotel before he could close his door. I love Danny Fox—he is truly my own dear brother—but his constant, irrepressible swagger could wear on you—especially after a few measly hours sleep—and his Connaught brogue came out full force when he was proper hung over.

He slumped back into the seat and lowered his glasses to glower at me. "Ye Gods! Yer wearing another one a them goddamn hats! Jaysus, Cole! Is there some store what sells the hats off old men's corpses? Get some style from yer ol' pal Foxy, eh? Let me at least send ye some designer threads from the piles of shite I get fer free."

"Behoove this sound of Irish sense," I growled in my best approximation of proper Irish. "Where the fuck are we going?"

"To the sea, lad. The snotgreen sea. The scrotum-tightening sea," he replied, nailing my Joyce with his own Joyce.

Smartass. Danny always managed to best me at my own clever games.

I adjusted the hat, just to spite him in my own ridiculous way. I wore the lime-green straw porkpie with a striped-tie band precisely because I knew he'd hate it.

Halfway down North Rodeo and heading for the Boulevard, I still didn't know where we were going. "All right, all right, forget the literary games. I do kind of need to know where in the hell we're going, Danny."

"It's 'Thunders' west of An Mhuir Cheilteach, mate."

"Pog mo thoin." I grumbled.

"Oh! Aye! And ye can kiss *my* sweet arse with tongue, ye bastard! Aye Aye, Cap'n. To Playa Del Ray!" Danny shouted.

I shook my head in disbelief. "You've got to be fucking kidding me! Playa Del Ray? I have a date at six, Danny. I have to be back *home* at six!"

He laughed and winked over his glasses. "Then I guess we'd best to be moving, young Master Cole!" He grabbed my hat and perched it just over his eyebrows.

I pulled out onto Santa Monica Boulevard and into the lunch-rush traffic jam that had probably started around dawn.

"Sooo, does this mean we are seeing the long and lovely redhead this evening?" he asked.

"If you didn't just bring me a huge cup of coffee, you'd be riding in the trunk."

"So that's a 'yes,' then?"

"We're not talking about her, Danny. And what the fuck was with getting me drunk off my ass and taking me to Eva's last night?'

He giggled in his mischievous, impish way and put his seat back, then yanked my hat down over his eyes. "Just tryin' to give ye a little taste of the good life, lad. I want ye to be happy. I know Eva's girls always make *me* happy."

"Oh yeah, *Big Red Shoes*!" I mocked.

He just laughed. "They had my bollocks caught in some damnable contraption I was strapped into! Didn't want me grapes turnin' sour! By the by, Eva was none too happy that ye left her unattended. Made me pay full price for breakfast."

I scowled at him, though I'm sure it didn't even register on his radar. He was busy admiring himself in the mirror on the visor and waving to the girls on the Boulevard.

There was a good minute's silence before he ventured another question. "This redhead — must be serious if ye pass up the Lady Eva for her, and then won't even talk about her with yer dearest, oldest pal."

I was getting flustered, just like he wanted. "Yeah, well, what's with the hookers at the hotel, huh?"

"Why, Mossimo Cole, ye right bastard. Those ladies were stewardesses, and very fine representatives of the service community, to be sure. Nudge, nudge, wink, wink."

"You are unbelievable."

"So they say, boyo. So they say."

"And trying to get me hammered? You know I can't drink anymore."

He sat bolt upright, defiant little boy ready to defend himself, jabbing a finger in my face. "You did that yeself, boyo! I didn't put those drinks in yer hand last night."

"Not all of them," I snarled back.

"No, not *all* of them." He let loose a loud guffaw and settled back down into his seat. "Fair enough, Mossy, fair enough. But ye weren't complaining. You're a big boy, and it's not that ye *can't* drink, ye choose not to. Last night ye decided... *otherwise*."

I took a long draw of my coffee — Irish as all hellfire. The cup had to be at least a quarter whiskey. I shoved it back at him. "Asshole."

He smirked at me from under the hat, giggled like a loon, and tossed his own empty cup out the window before sipping on the one I'd just returned.

Chapter 14

We pulled up in front of a dingy-looking duplex in the area they called *the Jungle*, right in front of the marina in Playa Del Ray. The garage door was open, and even from the car I could see that it was lined, floor to ceiling, with records.

I got out of the car, stretched and yawned before walking around the car to take my hat back from Danny, who hunched over to light a cigarette in his cupped hands. In the garage, hundreds, even thousands of cardboard sleeves cast the smell of vinyl and Windex heavy into the air. Small hand-drawn signs stated prices on various tables that held milk crates full of records and CDs.

"Hey, you can't fuckin' smoke in here, pal," came a thick South Boston accent.

Danny bobbed around to see where the voice was coming from, looking like a bad impression of Keith Richards, all dark glasses and messy hair as he mumbled unintelligibly.

"What? What's that then?" he stammered. He'd finished off both of our high-octane coffees on the way, and then dipped liberally into the flask hidden in his jacket. He was more or less soused.

"I said *no fuckin' smokin'* in here, *smaht* guy." The proprietor, a skinny white guy in track pants and a T-shirt, wore a dark blue ball cap backwards on his head.

I would have bet money it was a Red Sox cap, and I would have collected.

"We're looking for The Swede," I said, as if I didn't realize how ridiculous that sounded.

"Swede. Do I look fuckin' Swedish to you, kid? Does this sound like a Swedish fuckin' accent?"

Danny had stumbled outside and, after frantically sucking on his cigarette, tossed it out into the sand, and returned looking a little green.

"*Skogerbo!*" He shouted. "We must see Skogerbo! Olaf Skogerbo!"

"It's fuckin' Ollie, pal. Got it? Ollie!" The gentleman from Massachusetts was running out of patience.

"Look," I began.

"*Skogerbo!*" Danny continued to holler. "*We must see Skogerbo!*"

"Jesus Danny! Go sit in the car." I shoved him back into the sunshine.

He bawled like a scorched kitten.

"Always with the fuckin' 'Swede' shit. Fuck sakes! What the fuck do you want, anyways? Do I fuckin' know you two?"

"Ollie, my name is Cole, Moss Cole. I've been told you're the man to see about information on a very rare record."

"Moss Cole? What the fuck kinda name is fuckin' Moss?"

I sunk under the weight of the other half-million times I'd heard it.

He just eyeballed me up and down a few times, probably figuring me for an ex-rocker record exec, the hip kind that still wore band T-shirts and jeans every day—Henry Rollins with a Pasadena office space.

I shrugged off the question about my name. I'd been taking shit for it my whole life, and I hoped this guy would not be worth picking a fight. Between the drunken foulmouthed Irishman and the angry foulmouthed Southie, I would likely get nowhere... fast, and leave angry and frustrated.

I raised my hands in the universal gesture of peace. "The name is Italian. My full name is Mossimo Cole. I'm a detective."

He set down the album he'd been wiping off and took a step back toward the inner door. "Like a cop? You don't look like a cop, all that ink and your *smaht* fuckin' friend. Are you a fuckin' cop? Not that I got anything to fuckin' hide, mind you."

"Relax, I'm not a cop. I'm a private detective."

"Fuck off. Do they even have that anymore? Is that even a real fuckin' thing?"

"Yes. Yes it is." It was probably the seven-hundredth time that month I'd made that assertion.

"Does that explain that fuckin' hat? Come on, kid."

"Just a hat." I bit down on my cheek.

"Well, it's fuckin' atrocious, pal."

Usually on a Sunday, I'd be drinking some fine Antigua dark roast, listening to some jazz, maybe watching a movie. This was much better. I reminded myself to get a new line of work for the three-hundredth time that week.

"Ollie, I want to know if you've heard anything about an ultra-rare Sinatra pressing. Private recording from the Mozambique in '48?"

He eyeballed me carefully before speaking. "You got some ID, private dick?"

I pulled out my wallet and flashed the badge and State ID card. He looked at it closely, then gave me another once-over before biting his bottom lip and stepping back to the counter, trying to manage *casual* and pulling off something closer to *extreme unease*.

"So you sellin' or buyin', pal?"

"I'm just trying to return it to the owner."

Ollie laughed and doubled over in mock theatricality—a terrible actor. "Oh, that's a good one. That's fuckin' wicked hilarious, pal!"

He continued to laugh, wiping at fake tears and sobbing to catch his breath.

"Look, man," I said, holding back the urge to haul him over the counter. "I just want to know if you've heard of this bloody record, okay?"

Skogerbo collected himself, looked me up and down, then turned his back and went back to cleaning records.

"Ain't nothin' in that for me, pal. Sounds like bullshit, anyways. There was a recording ban in '48." He took pains to avoid my very best impatient stare. "I think maybe you just collect your drunken mick and fuck off."

Danny had stumbled quietly back into the shop and had begun digging through the piles of records labelled "A," no doubt searching for some of his own *Atomic Sphinkters* albums.

Now he slunk quietly up behind Skogerbo and cuffed him behind the ear. "Who are ye calling a drunken mick? Ye bean-lickin' Boston wannabe-Irish sodomite man-whore *cocksucker*!"

Skogerbo spun around to face Danny. The two of them got chest to chest like a couple of coaches at a Red Sox/Yankees game, and started screaming into each other's red faces in a steady stream of invective liberally interspersed with *fooks* and *facks*.

Danny asserted that all Bostonians wished they were real Irishmen.

Skogerbo retorted that Ireland was a "bitch-rock full of terrorists, whores and monkey-faced, drunken leprechauns, who were not even fit for mascots at Boston's St. Paddy's Day parade."

The classy debate reminded me of the kind usually hurled back and forth across the hood of a car while stuck at a light in the sketchier part of North Hollywood.

The whole ugly affair ended when Skogerbo finally recognized the infamous Foxy Thunders and stopped dead in his tracks to vigorously shake Danny's hand, and to ask for a picture and if he would sign a few records. The whole thing unfolded like an especially surreal, and thoroughly profane, *Three Stooges* bit.

"Only if ye answer my friend Cole's questions," Danny told him, smirking like one of the aforementioned monkey-faced leprechauns.

"All right, all right," Skogerbo relented. "Ask away, Mike Hammer."

"I just want to know if you've heard of this Sinatra record or anybody trying to sell it." Tired, exasperated, and fed up with bull-headed loudmouths with thick accents, I wanted to go home and sleep before my date with the divine Rosie Stetch.

Ollie dug through a shelf at the front of his store and pulled out a stack of notebooks. He dug through those until he found a battered green-covered loose-leaf number, and flipped halfway through the book until he found what he was looking for.

"I had a few guys call about that record, couple of 'em sayin' they'd pay top fuckin' dollar. I tried to tell 'em that it's probably a joke. If that record was out there, Sinatra himself would have had it and released it six ways from Sunday. Ain't nobody knew the game like Frankie Blue Eyes. I told 'em, but this one guy, *Testicles* or something—"

"Testaverde," I corrected.

"Yeah, that's it. I can barely read my own writing, y'know—how'd you know that? You working for that fuckin guy?" He backed away again. He'd clearly been exposed to Joey Thumbs' usual charming banter.

"No, I'm not working for him. He's a thug, works for a guy named DeFrancesco. Vegas mob."

"I thought they chased the fuckin' mob outta Vegas."

I guessed that Skogerbo had never been mistaken for Ernest Hemingway. And I was really enjoying how everyone thought they knew better than the professional investigator. Just like Rodney Dangerfield, I got no respect.

"Who else?" I asked.

"I gotta worry about this fuckin' mob guy?"

"Just don't tell him anything you do find out about the record. Probably best not to mention me, either."

He looked nervously back and forth between Danny and me, obviously weighing the increased value of half a dozen signed Atomic Sphinkters albums against the possibility of Godfather-like reprisals.

"I, uh, I already told him what I fuckin' knew! He said he'd fuckin' check back! Am I fuckin' hooped? Those guys like to cut off your balls. I happen to fuckin' like my fuckin' balls, pal!" He got more profane the more worked up he became.

"Joey Testaverde is a scumbag. He just likes scaring people. He's not going to bother you unless he thinks you have the record. Get it?"

"Yeah," he replied with no small amount of nervousness. "I'm out of the fuckin' Sinatra market."

"So who else called about it?"

"Some guy tellin' me he was Obie fuckin' Stetch, legendary fuckin' record producer Obie Stetch? You believe that?"

"Yeah, he's a miserable, senile old prick. And yes, that was him on the phone. What else?"

He dug through the notebooks again and came up with a brown cover. Much flipping ensued. It didn't look like much of a filing system to me, but it seemed to work.

"Yeah, right here. Fuckin' Sinatra. 1948. The Mozambique. They say Lady Ella sat in on *Stormy Weather* and *La Vie En Rose*. That woulda been magic, kid!" He smiled.

My patience with our new Southie friend reached a new low. "Tell me what I don't know."

"Right. Fuckin' relax, pal. Right here. Stetch told me it was a single press 78, cut from the original wax press, which was destroyed. Fuckin' shame. He also said it had twelve tracks, six per side, but Ella only came up for the last two. Fuckin' guy went on and on. Fuckin'."

I shook my head in disbelief. Who swore like that? Seriously?

"Anything that would help me find the record for Stetch? You help me find it, I bring Foxy back in a couple of weeks and you can set up a signing. I also happen to know Belinda Michaels and Charlie Moses."

"Fuck off! You know Charlie fuckin' Moses? Charlie Moses who played the fuckin' Long Bar with fuckin' Duke? Charlie Moses who backed Miles Davis on the fuckin' *'58 Sessions*?"

"Yeah. Charlie Moses."

"Who the fuck *are* you, pal?" He was looking at me like I was the face of Jesus Christ smoking on his grilled cheese. "Hells fuckin' yeah! All right. You got yourself a fuckin' deal. The other guy said his name was Jorge. Called asking what the sticker on something like that record would be. I told him all depends on the fuckin' buyer, y'know. Could be ten grand, could be fuckin' two-fifty...."

"Two hundred and fifty? *Thousand*?" said Danny. "Jaysus!"

"Did this Jorge leave a number or anything? You see him in the flesh?" I asked.

"Hang on, hang on," Skogerbo stammered, digging through yet another notebook. "He fuckin' left his number. It's in here some fuckin' place. Hang on. Fuckin'."

I stifled a laugh.

Danny did not follow suit. He cackled and slapped Skogerbo on the back. "Fuck me, son. Where'd ye learn to bloody curse like that? Just throwin' it on the end of a fucking sentence! That's bloody brilliant, that is!"

Ollie stared at Danny, a glossy vacuousness slopped across his face.

I decided to step in before another altercation started. "Foxy, would you mind waiting in the car? I'll be done in a couple of minutes and we'll get you some lunch, all right?"

Danny gave me a questioning glance, but shrugged it off and stumbled off through the garage and out into the sunlight. He faltered at the doorway when the bright midday sun hit him, as if he'd taken a left hook and was about to take the mat to the face. He shambled for a second, grappling to get his sunglasses open and over his poor nocturnal eyes. Once he had the shades on and straightened himself up, he spun like a quick draw cowboy, shooting his index fingers out at Skogerbo.

"See ye 'round, Boston!" he laughed. "*Fuckin'*!" Then he shambled off into the blinding light of the afternoon sun.

Skogerbo shot me another dirty look. "Maybe ya don't bring that fuckin' retard back here. He's fuckin' irritating."

"No problem."

He gave me the number and a brief rundown of the conversation, and I bought all the copies he had of Foxy Thunders and the Atomic Sphinkters records. I planned to force Danny to sign them and then *donate* them back to Mr. Skogerbo's collection. I gave him my card and reassured him that Joey Testaverde was not to worry about, so long as he didn't think Skogerbo had the record. He seemed placated by that obvious lie, so I let it go and headed back to the car. I needed to get home in time for my date.

Christ, is that what it is? When's the last time I was on a date? And with the kid there too?

I must have been losing my goddamn mind. I was nervous. I'd never been nervous about a date before. I needed coffee—real coffee, sans the Irish sidekick. I also needed to ditch my own Irish sidekick as soon as possible and get back home.

Chapter 15

Danny had fallen asleep in the car, so I started up and headed back toward Santa Monica to get him back to the hotel before he woke up and caused me any more grief. I made it to Century City before he woke up swearing at me and insisting on lunch.

"It's 4 PM, Danny. You can get something to eat at the hotel."

"Fine way to treat the man who found the man who got ye the goods. Fuckin' fuckin' fuckin'!" He laughed and scowled at me at the same time, which for anyone else would have been a mean feat.

"Yeah, you also had the guy ready to toss us out on our asses."

"But ye got yer number, my son. Did ye not?"

"Yeah, yeah. Thank you, Danny. Now will you promise me? Please just go in the hotel, eat something, and go to sleep for a few days?'

"Sure, anything for ye, old brotherman."

As we passed Wilshire, a black SUV peeled around the corner and came up quick behind us, swerving out to pace us in the adjoining lane. I looked over as one of the black windows came down to reveal a young Asian man in a black suit and black glasses gesturing for me to pull over.

"I think that fella wants a word with ye, Cole." Danny finished off his flask and hurled it out the window at the black beast that was pacing us. "*Fuck off, ye cunts!*" he hollered, falling back in spasms of laughter against the passenger-side door.

The SUV wove ever so slightly into our lane, nudging me over toward the curb. I calculated ahead and tried to gauge the foot traffic and tight corner on Roxbury. When I hit that corner, I pulled hard right, skidding the little car with a screech and feeling my side lift, barely perceptible, and bounce on solid tires. It took me a second to right our course and pull into a lane.

Danny jumped in his seat and shouted "*Hallelujah!*" before noticing we were going the wrong way on a one-way street. The hallelujahs quickly evolved to a string of high-volume cursing, Danny's hands glued firmly to the dash.

I swerved in and out of lanes, dodging the oncoming flood of metal and shocked humanity, and made it a couple of quick blocks before pulling it hard into a parking garage. I used an old handbrake-slide trick to throw us behind a delivery truck and out of sight from the street.

"Well fuck!" Danny exclaimed. "That was goddamn impressive, Cole!"

"Shhhh, Danny! Shut up," I said in a hushed grumble.

Seconds later the black SUV crept into the garage and proceeded to prowl past us. The black and chrome nose of the thing edged into sight as I pulled Danny down under the dash, hoping beyond hope that they'd either miss the car or think we'd bailed.

Then came the sound of three doors opening and slamming shut.

I held my breath and closed my eyes, trying to focus myself for whatever was going to happen next.

"Mr. Cole?" Husky, deep, and with a considerable Japanese accent. "We wish to speak to Mossimo Cole. You come out now and we will have no trouble."

Right. That's how these things usually play out. I stood slowly and stepped from the shadow of the car with my hands out in front of me, palms up, in the universal sign of *'Please don't shoot me in the face.'*

Four Japanese dudes in matching black suits and shades flanked the SUV, each with one hand in the lapel of their jackets—never a good omen. A thin, tall gentleman stood out front and center, with a bald-headed wall of a man standing at attention to his right.

"Mossimo Cole," the bald one demanded in his rough grumble.

"I'm Cole." I displayed as much nonchalance as I could manage. "What can I do for you gentlemen?"

"First, you have your companion come out where we can see him," growled Baldy.

"Danny, come on out. It's all right."

I nodded towards him to come out from behind the car, while still holding my hands up.

Pounding steps on metal followed, and then Danny came flying out from above, landing in a ridiculous kung fu stance he probably picked up in a '70s exploitation flick. He started caterwauling like Bruce Lee and jabbing at the air, swinging his feet in high, wide arcs toward the men by the SUV. They smirked at first, but when his foot came a little too close to one of the wingmen, he dealt Danny a powerhouse *choku zuki* punch, square in his balls, as he twisted through the air like some kind of drunk whirlwind. He fell to the ground like a 200-pound bag of dirt. The resounding *thud* accompanied a gasping yelp reminiscent of a poodle yanked across the room by her neck.

I went slowly to Danny to make sure he was okay, and helped him to his feet. His face was turning purple as he gulped for air like a koi fish out of water. He wretched once and spit out a stream of whiskey-scented bile, then took a huge gasping breath and bellowed one long vowel sound at the top of his lungs.

"Mr. Cole," the thin one called. "You should control your friend. We do not appreciate these antics. We have business to discuss with *you*. He is of no concern to us. He would be wise to quiet himself." His voice was elegant and refined, highly educated, which I read as "smart and dangerous."

Danny stood himself up straight and turned to point a finger at the thin man.

I turned him away hard and shoved him back toward the car, warning him with a harsh whisper. "Danny! Shut the hell up before you get us killed."

He held himself up against the side of the car as I stepped toward the thin man. "I apologize. My friend has had too much liquor and forgets his place easily."

"This isn't some movie where we all speak in stilted *Eengrish,* Mr. Cole."

"Of course. I'm sorry, but—you seem to have me at a loss."

He eyeballed me with a sharp look, as much taking in my details and deducing my worth as putting me in my place.

"My name is Ken Nakadaka. I represent Mr. Takahashi Kenzo of the Oyabun Corporation."

I knew the name, and that's what the thin man was testing me for. Kenzo was a high-up in the Yakuza. In the Mafia, they would have called him a consiglieri or advisor. And *Oyabun* was one of the names Yakuza gave themselves, like Sicilian Mafia call themselves La Cosa Nostra. In my experience, one didn't play around with the Yakuza, so I figured I'd just come straight to the point.

"You mean the *saiko komon* of the Yakuza? That Takahashi Kenzo?"

"Very good, Mr. Cole. Since you know of our organization and our ways, you should be much more receptive to our... *requests.*"

"What does a Yakuza advisor want with little old me? That's the question."

Danny was mumbling threats under his breath behind me. I was hoping to God that these men had a decent sense of humor or a poor grasp of Irish profanity.

Nakadaka nodded to the bald man, who retrieved a briefcase from the back seat of the SUV and laid it out on the hood of the car. He snapped it open to reveal enough cash to choke Godzilla himself.

"This is one million dollars, Mr. Cole. My employer would very much like to give you this money in exchange for a certain item you are tracking for the Las Vegas Italians."

"Fuckin' hell," Danny gushed from behind me.

"You're after the record? One million dollars for a record? What the hell is the matter with you people?"

"Mr. Kenzo is a great admirer of Mr. Sinatra, and would very much like to add this recording to his collection."

"Well, like I told Joey Thumbs—your *Vegas Italian*—I don't know where it is or how to get it. It's still a question whether it even really exists. The man who says he lost it is very old and most likely out of his mind."

"It is real, Mr. Cole, to be sure. Mr. Kenzo has heard this recording at the charity of your Mr. Stetch and has previously made offers equaling this one for its sale. Mr. Stetch declined those offers, so now we make the same offer to you. Find the record, deliver it to me, and we will be glad to give you this reward."

Danny piped up from behind me, his tempers recovered from the shot to the balls. "And if he doesn't find it? Or if he gives it back to Stetch? Then what? Ye chop him up with one of yer fancy swords there? Feed him to the koi fish?"

"Danny," I said quietly. "I swear to Christ. Please don't help. Shut up. Shut up and get in the fucking car. Right now."

I watched out of the corner of my eye to make sure he was backing off. When the car door slammed, I turned my attention back to Nakadaka.

Baldie was shoving the case into the back seat.

"We are not like the Italians, Mr. Cole. If you don't deliver the item, we will not punish you. Keep in mind, however, that we will do whatever is necessary to acquire the item that our employer has sent us here for. Do you understand?"

"Yeah, I get it. You won't kill me for stiffing you on the record, but you will kill me to find out where it is."

"You speak very plainly, Mr. Cole. I respect that. I hope that we can be amiable with each other. You could prove valuable to our organization, if you play your cards properly." He held out a hand to shake.

I took it. Then I laid it on the line. "I'll speak plainly then. I don't work for criminals or thugs—Italian or Japanese. And I don't take threats lying down. I know your reputation, Nakadaka, as I'm sure you know mine. Let's leave it at that." I said it in Japanese, just to drive the point home.

He bowed and took a card from inside his jacket and handed it to me. "If you change your mind, Mr. Cole."

I took the card and bowed, keeping my eyes on his.

He nodded and stepped into the SUV as the other doors slammed shut almost simultaneously.

I had my hand on the door handle when something went *thwock* into the hood and Danny jumped like a scared squirrel in the front seat. The sound of raucous, guttural laughter exploded behind me as the SUV pulled forward, and Nakadaka leaned out the passenger window. I kept my eyes on the shiny metal star poking out of the front of my car.

"One last thing, Mr. Cole—a piece of advice. Mr. Sinatra aligned himself with the Mafia. It was a very big mistake for him, and it will prove equally unfortunate for you."

My shoulders sagged under the weight of all of the bullshit. How in the hell did I get mixed up in this ridiculous movie-of-the-week? I pried the shuriken loose from the hood and walked casually towards the SUV.

I tossed it in the open window, shaking my head. "Seriously?"

As I walked away with my back to them, half-expecting to feel the red-hot sting of steel between my aching shoulders and my favorite neck, the vehicle roared to life and headed out of the garage. I sank back into the shadows to ponder what else could possibly add to this shitstorm.

Danny sat, arms crossed like a petulant kid. Poor baby.

I sat hunched on a concrete pylon, wishing I'd never left home yesterday, wishing I'd never left Eva's last night, wishing I was somebody—*anybody*—else.

***

"A million fuckin' dollars, Cole! That'd buy a whole lot of stupid hats, boyo!"

"Shut the fuck up, Danny." I slid in behind the wheel and started the car.

"Hey, I was just tryin' to have yer back. Million bucks doesn't mean fuck-all to me, lad. Be nice for ye though. Take yer ginger lady on a trip, buy that little one a nanny so ye have more time for knockin' the boots... No need to be sore at me. I'm the one got punched in the bollocks, remember? I would have had that little cocksucker if he didn't fuckin' sucker-punch me in the mala. Who the fuck punches ye in the bollocks in a bloody kung fu fight? Fuckin' amateurs... Bruce Lee never punched a fella in the berries...."

He never did quit talking. I dropped him off a few minutes later and watched him weave towards the lobby. He stopped at the door and dropped his pants to shake his ass at me, before two security officers lifted him by the arms and whisked him out of view. He'd be fine, once they realized who he was. Danny had been pulling shit like that every day of his life, and he hardly ever needed my help to get out of it.

I headed home, hoping to make good enough time to re-dress myself and call in a couple of favors. Maybe I'd even call up the mysterious Jorge and have a quick pot of coffee. At least I didn't get the shit kicked out of me this time—a pleasant new development. How long it would last was another matter entirely. Joey Thumbs was sure to come calling soon, and probably not alone.

Chapter 16

"Menlowe? It's Cole. You boys use a little work?"

"We're always up for a little fun. What do you need, a spanking? Maybe some handcuffs?"

I sipped calmly at my bowl of latte before answering, just to let him know I was serious. "Joey Thumbs. You hear anything else from that camp, or had a chance to relay my message?"

"Oh, I told him. He was very unimpressed. Tightly wound, that one. And more than a little bit of a psycho."

"What happened?"

"Oh, he gave us an angry little tirade and threatened to have us killed, all the usual macho *paisan* bullshit. Then he said to give you a message in return. He said to tell you that he would get you *one way or the other*. Very Wicked Witch of the West. That man has a lot of issues."

"You have no idea," I replied. "I guess having you two shadow him and tell me what he's up to is out of the question now?"

"Well, I guess that depends on how you ask that question, now doesn't it?"

"Five hundred make a good start?"

"That's a start, but certainly not a happy ending."

"All right, five each. A thousand dollars. But you stay on him. I want a report once you're on him and then every three hours, got me?"

"Sure, honey. I get you."

I hung up and ruminated, momentarily, on how fast I was running myself out of business with all of these payouts and bribes when I didn't really have a client or a solid plan for a payoff. Of course, the numbers were getting bigger all the time. That also entailed getting into bed with the mob and the Yakuza, either one of which would cut it off just as soon as play with it.

I pulled on my boots and grabbed a sport coat from the closet, topping it with Pops' fedora, then took my coffee out to the front step.

Rosie pulled up just after six, and I tucked my cup under a bush next to the steps and sauntered over to the car. Holly was in the back, looking every bit the princess in a little pink dress with black polka dots and tiny black Mary Janes on her feet. She waved to me and I waved back, and was about to plant my ass in the passenger seat when Rosie asked if I wanted to drive.

I wasn't sure what the deal was, but didn't want to disappoint her, so I quickly hustled to her side of the car. She was already getting out, but I was trying vainly to grasp at chivalry, so I practically sprinted to the passenger side to open the door for her.

Once the game of musical chairs was over, and we were rolling away from the curb, I asked, "So where are we going this evening, ladies?"

"Babalu? It's on Montana and 10th. Santa Monica."

Unbelievable. Back to Santa Monica. What a day. I knew the place: Caribbean fusion. It looked like a little stucco fish shack, but inside it was tin ceilings and bamboo. They had mismatched kitchen tables out on the sidewalk as a patio, and they made a great chicken Stella.

"Thanks for driving," Rosie said after a long and somewhat awkward pause in conversation. "I hate driving, but you live in L.A., you can't really live without it, right?"

Unfortunately true.

"I've always wished we could live someplace small and quiet, some little village where everything was walking or bike-riding distance, a nice quiet town—slow and easy—no traffic, no cell phones. *God*! I hate cell phones!"

My hand slipped into my jacket pocket and fumbled with the power button on my phone without my prior consent.

"The worst, the absolute worst," she continued, "are the scuzzy yuppie hipsters in designer suits hitting on you everywhere you go." She blushed, just a little. "I guess you wouldn't know about that."

I felt a colony of butterflies take wing in the pit of my stomach, so I gave an awkward chuckle. "You'd be surprised how often a schlub like me gets propositioned by scuzzy yuppie hipsters."

She laughed again, a beautiful, booming, full and completely un-self-conscious sound.

I noticed a car, two back, following each of our turns and keeping an exact distance between us. I made a mental note to keep an eye on it. I was about to turn my attention back to the wonderful Stetch girls when the faint yet unmistakable strains of *Strangers in the Night* warbled through the radio. I began fumbling with increasing panic at the dials on the dashboard, inadvertently turning it up just as Frank began to sing.

"...EXCHANGING GLANCES....

"...WOND'RING IN THE NIGHT, WHAT WERE THE CHANCES...."

Rosie rambled on about Sinatra as if I hadn't heard every story out there already. "You know the funniest thing Dad used to say about Sinatra? How he had such delicate hands. Dad would use awful words like *queer* and *pussy*"

I glanced at the rear-view mirror, and the young girl in the back seat, my discomfort thumping in my ears.

Rosie continued, unaware of the hard eye I was giving the damned radio dial. "Anyway, I think he was always enthralled how Frank was so manly and tough, yet so gentle at the same time."

"...WE'D BE SHARING LOVE...."

"...BEFORE THE NIGHT...."

I was on the verge of putting my fist through the goddamn thing when Rosie reached out and clicked it off.

"I... umm... I'm sorry," I said. "I just can't take any more Sinatra."

"It's okay." She smiled and laid her hand on top of mine on the stick shift.

"I like when he sings *Obee Doobee Doobee*," Holly added from the back seat.

"Sorry, kid. I feel like I've been hearing it all week, y'know?"

"It's okay, Mr. Cole."

The smile stretched across my face without warning at her sing-song little voice, so proper and polite. It drained the fury and the panic out of me in an instant. Is that what kids did to you? How they made tough-guy twenty-year-olds into soft, lawn-mowing thirty-year-old daddies?

"You can call me Moss, Holly."

"Right. Like on a tree."

"It's short for Mossimo. It's Italian."

For the first time in about twenty years, that explanation didn't grate on me like a quarter in a coffee grinder. I smiled at Holly in the mirror, then snuck another look for our shadow.

"So, *Mossimo* Cole, what do you love about L.A.?" Rosie's slender fingers wove through my callous, weathered stumps.

"To tell you the truth, I've lived all over the world, in little towns and big cities. Los Angeles is usually my least favorite of all of them. Right now it's my very favorite place to be." I hazarded a glance in her direction, and was rewarded with the sight of a blush rising in her cheeks, and a coquettish turn toward the window to keep me from seeing it.

"You are cheesy macaroni, Monsmemmo," came the giggling criticism from the back.

"Holly!" Rosie admonished.

"It's all right. I am indeed, *I macaroni e formaggio*." I looked in the rear-view mirror to catch Holly's look of disbelief.

"*E Scuza, bambina*," I continued. "*Parli Italiano?*"

Her eyes were wide, and her face full of that lovely innocence and shock that only children could display; that thing that made them so special: a lack of sufficient disappointment with the world.

"Perhaps in Gaelic? German? *Parlez-vous Francais*? Portuguese, *talvez?*"

Her eyes seemed to get wider and wider with each new language.

"Ahh! *¿Quizás usted habla español?*"

"*Si?*" came the tiny voice from the back seat, accompanied by another peal of her mother's glorious laughter.

"He's just teasing, Honey. I don't think Mr. Cole really speaks all of those languages."

I gave her my best incredulous sideways stare, while trying to keep my eyes on the road.

"Ye of little faith! I take great offense to that, m'lady. I do, in fact, speak eight languages. Fluently."

I caught Holly in the back seat counting on her fingers and silently mouthing the names of the ones I'd already used.

"That was only six." She stated with a surplus of confidence.

"*Hai! Soreha hontou dearu.*"

If her eyes got any wider, they would eclipse the rest of her head. "What language was that?" she asked breathlessly.

"Japanese, kiddo. I also speak a little Mandarin Chinese." I smiled.

"Wow! You must be really, really, really smart!"

"I do okay. But I bet you're much smarter than I'll ever be."

She blushed just like her Mama and tucked her chin into her shoulder.

"Sweet talker, you are," Rosie said, reaching over and taking my hand.

I could really get used to these two.

The mystery car passed us as I slowed to turn past the restaurant. We pulled up on the street just down the block from Babalu, and I helped Holly out of the back seat with a bow. They each took one of my hands and led me to the corner. The restaurant stood like a weird tiny stucco church, plaster palm fronds flanking the door and garish flags and curtains flapping lightly in the soft breeze.

The warm night's lovely sunset had just begun, so Holly asked if we could sit outside.

The waiter, a surprisingly snooty Cuban named Arturo, demonstrated the requisite false manners and snotty attitude of a Beverly Hills maître d', despite his ridiculously stereotypical getup: flamenco pants and flowing white shirt, unbuttoned to display his thicket of chest hair, and sashed at the waist with a red scarf. A single dainty gold crucifix adorned his neck, and he was actually wearing Cuban-heeled boots, not to mention the pencil-thin moustache readily visible beneath his constantly upturned nose.

I wondered if I was wearing too much cologne, as he seemed deeply offended by my presence. I ordered a bottle of house red and a 7-Up for Holly, and Arturo strutted off into the place.

He must have had other things to attend to, since we didn't see him again for twenty minutes. When he did finally return, we had been having a rousing conversation about world travel. He set the drinks down and the wine glasses, then stood impatiently waiting for us to order. I felt like making him wait the same twenty minutes, but instead I gestured for him to ask the ladies what they'd like.

Rosie, as most women do on first dates, ordered a salad.

I had Holly convinced to try fried plantains with her turkey burger, and she swore she would share whatever I had. I asked for the crab enchiladas and a side of the yam fries they made with cayenne buttermilk sauce.

Arturo sighed heavily and gave me a fish-eyed look, as if I was wasting his life by even being there. Whatever I'd done to him in a past life, must have been a doozy. I warned Holly that Arturo didn't like me, so she'd probably want to stay away from my coconut rice and waiter spit. The kid laughed, but Rosie warned me with a raised eyebrow of disapproval. I shrugged it off hoping my charming effervescence would win her over in the end.

Rosie sat there with her flowing auburn locks tumbling down over her shoulders, and the green and gold flowered sundress that flowed over her curves so delicately, and I had a hard time not thinking of the plump softness of those lips pressed against mine. I strained to suppress the inevitable impure thoughts in light of my other present company.

The food came—eventually—and we saw very little of Arturo. We had a delightful dinner, a nice conversation. Some of it was about me, some about them, a lot of it about Holly's trip to Lego Land, apparently the West Coast Mecca for children her age. Disneyland was passé, and the zoos and aquariums were old hat.

A warm, comfortable feeling overtook me, being with these two people, as if they had always been missing from my life and we had just now found each other, and needed to make up for lifetimes apart. I'd never known this kind of bliss, outside of playing my trumpet or tinkling alone on the piano in the Hi-Lo with the moonlight bouncing off the ivories.

When Arturo finally made another appearance, we were ready for some of their infamous coconut praline pie and some coffee — cinnamon cocoa for little Miss Lego Land.

Arturo nodded and half-heartedly picked up our plates.

That's when the rumble rose behind us.

Chapter 17

Two cars came up fast, roaring to a stop at the intersection. The unmistakable clicks and clacks of chambers being racked got me immediately out of my seat, toppling the table to block the line of fire between the girls and the road, and hauling them both down to crouch behind it.

The shots rang out *rat-a-tat* like a furious drum solo amplified by the gods of thunder. I held Rosie tight to me, with Holly tucked into my chest. If they were getting her, they were going through me first. The explosions of gunfire boomed around us, sending shards of stone tabletop and stucco singing through the air.

Arturo flew off his feet and landed on his back with a thud. Holly screamed, and I reached out to drag him behind the table with us. In a heartbeat, the air filled with silence as the cars screamed off down Montana Avenue.

I rushed to my knees, poked my head out from behind the table, and watched them squeal around a corner — two dark, late-model sedans, the kind Joey Thumbs and his friends employed for their more nefarious outings, one of them suspiciously similar to the car that had followed us earlier.

I turned back to Rosie, who tore the tablecloth out from under the overturned table, wadded it up, and pressed it against Arturo's chest. A horrible wet sucking sound, like a vacuum cleaner in six inches of water, came from under the cloth. Arturo's face had turned pallid and sickly.

I looked at Holly, her face a mask of shock and fear, and pulled her close to me. I put my hand on Rosie's shoulder and spoke as calmly as possible, directly into her ear. My ears were ringing like church bells, and I couldn't imagine hers were doing much better.

"I'll help him. Take Holly inside and make sure they're calling an ambulance."

She looked confused, but after looking from me to the stricken face of her daughter, and staring at Arturo struggling for breath and drowning in his own blood right in front of her, she snapped out of it and drew her baby girl to her breast.

"It's okay, Honey. Everything is okay. Come on, we'll go inside and call a doctor. Daddy—" She stopped herself and gave me a quick, startled glance. "Mr. Cole will help this man, okay? Come on, baby. Come on."

They crawled out from the maelstrom of broken tables and torn earth and scrabbled to their feet, running inside while looking left and right, cringing at the fear of more bullets flying around them.

I turned my attention to the dying man and moved the cloth. He had a thumb-sized hole about three inches under his right clavicle. It was sucking in air and bubbling with blood. I put the palm of my hand over it to, hoping to seal the wound until help came. I struggled to remember my police academy training and, keeping one hand on his chest, used the other to feel around for something better than my sweaty palm to block the hole. I found nothing nearby.

As red foam trickled out between my fingers, I reached into my jacket pocket and flipped my wallet out onto the ground, fumbling in the folds until I found what I was looking for. Arturo saw what was in my hand and his eyes widened. I'm not sure what he thought I was going to do to that hole in his chest, but he soon relented and sank back with a groan—whether from loss of blood, shock, or the realization that I was trying to save his life by sealing the hole with the malleable condom package.

After what seemed like hours, sirens blared in the distance. The wailing cry of the ambulance got closer and louder, then steady, until a hand on my back nudged me aside so the paramedics could get to Arturo. I stumbled back against one of the palm trees behind me and vainly tried to tell them what was wrong with him.

One of the paramedics took my arm and led me into the restaurant, where Rosie and Holly huddled together in the corner. He sat me down and manhandled me to be sure I was just boggled and not shot.

Holly ran to me with the remains of Pops' hat in her hands. "Here, Mosbesso, I found your hat," she said, big teary eyes looking for something. She held it out to me like some sad discovery.

I looked down at the crumpled wad of felt, missing chunks in at least three spots where bullets meant for my head had bounced it across the lawn. My heart cracked in twelve places as I remembered all of the times Pops had worn that hat, all the times he'd flipped it onto my head when it was so big that it would cover my face to my nose. Tears welled up as the pain flooded my chest.

Pops. Daddy. She called me Daddy.

"Thank you, Holly." I smiled as warmly as I could manage, still fighting the tears in my eyes, clutching the remains of Pops' favorite hat so hard that my fingers ached.

Then she jumped into my lap and threw her little arms around my neck. I wasn't quite sure what to do, but I put my arms around her and held her tight, vainly praying to take the last twenty minutes away, knowing it would forever be reflected in her eyes.

Rosie came to sit next to me and, with tears in her eyes, mouthed the words *thank you*.

I smiled weakly and dropped my eyes. I never should have let them sit outside. I knew those monsters were following us. *Daddy.* I never thought Thumbs would try something like that. *Daddy?* What in the hell was I getting myself into? *Daddy.* Could I be a husband? A father? Neither of those things had ever crossed my addled brain.

As I looked down at Holly, still clinging to me for comfort and protection, a solid, flaming ball of rage began growing where that pain had hollowed out my chest mere moments before. Joey Thumbs was going to pay for this. He was going to pay in pain and blood, and he was going to know that he was being sent straight to hell in the name of this little girl.

The police arrived moments later and, when I asked to leave to take the girls home, they told me to sit and wait. The gang unit and a couple of homicide detectives were on their way to speak to me. I had a bad feeling about who they meant.

I set Rosie and Holly up in a back booth, and had the manager bring them new desserts and cocoa, while I pleaded my case to the uniforms.

"Look, we just came for dinner, and some gangbangers started shooting up the place. Maybe they were after the waiter."

"Yeah, sure. Just sit down and wait, Mr. Cole. The detectives were very specific that we not let you out of our sight."

Shit. That nailed it. Lincoln and McGuire.

I'd barely registered the thought when the door opened and two of L.A.'s finest detectives stomped through the door. I had been perfectly happy to tip them off that the mob was in town, but I sure as hell didn't want to find myself cooking under their nuclear heat lamp.

"Goddamn it, Cole! What'd you get into this time?" came the deep bellow from somewhere in the expansive chest of George McGuire.

At six-and-a-half feet tall and something close to the mass of Pluto, he might not quite make planet status, but he was a solid rock of a man with a brain and manners to match. What he lacked in intelligence and wit, he made up for in cruelty and anger management issues. McGuire probably spent his personal time polishing guns and breaking things with his nightstick. His partner, Lacy Lincoln, despite her stripper name and curvaceous yet tiny body, was all kinds of clever and single-minded in her dedication to putting bad guys away. Together they made the single greatest cop that never lived. They were the long arm of the Organized Crimes Division, the place where angry, neck-breaking cops go to get their jollies, beating down Crips and Bloods and chasing down Vietnamese gangbangers in souped-up Honda Civics. They also dealt with the more classic gangsters, like our friend Joey Thumbs and his boss.

I knew I should have called them in, but I was trying to... well, shit, I didn't know what the fuck I was doing anymore.

Lincoln sauntered over to where I was sitting, and leaned over the table, pushing her elbows in to enhance her already impressive cleavage. She stared straight into my eyeballs, daring me to look down her shirt and give her a reason to sick McGuire on me.

I glanced helplessly back to Rosie and Holly, who were completely unawares and sitting silent and morose, both staring into their cups. I took a breath and mentally prepared to defend myself. I turned my head back, careful to keep my eyes above board, and brought my coffee cup to my lips, taking a long slurp of joe before I spoke.

"Lacy. Nice of you to bring your friends for a visit." I nodded downward without looking. "And McGuire. Have you lost weight, Georgie boy?" I smirked and put the cup down, still careful not to stare into the abyss of Lacy's Teutonic neckline, begging to be unleashed on the world like a global disaster.

McGuire stepped behind me, his shadow moving in front of him like freezing night moving over a desert. It was like standing outside during an eclipse. Once he was directly over top of me, and simultaneously surrounding me on all sides, I put my head back to stare straight up at him as his shadow swallowed me whole.

Lacy pulled out a chair and sat neatly across from me, crossing her legs to the side of the chair and flipping her stylishly bobbed, two-tone blond hair from her shoulders. She leaned back and flashed her million-dollar smile.

"Not falling for the ol' *tits 'n' giggles* bit today, eh, Cole?" she asked. Lacy's voice had gravel in it, the kind of voice you'd expect from a sixty-year-old woman who favored whiskey and pall malls. There was a time I had found that voice very sexy.

"Not today, kitten. I've had a long night and I have two ladies to escort home. Maybe next time. Besides, I wouldn't want your pet rhino here to get jealous and start removing things, like my arms."

"Well, Cole," she replied, "you seem to have that effect with the dudes, no? I hear you had a little trouble with Joey Thumbs a few days ago. Could this—" She waved her arms toward the street for clarification. "—have anything to do with that?"

"You'd have to ask Mr. Thumbs, I guess. I was just having a nice dinner with my friends over there." I nodded towards Rosie and Holly in the back. "I heard two cars tear-ass down the street toward us and slam on the brakes, followed by some clickety-clacks. I didn't wait around to ask them who they came to see."

McGuire put two gigantic hands, roughly the size, shape and weight of two full-grown English bulldogs, on my shoulders and began to squeeze.

Pain like nothing I'd ever experienced shot through my injured shoulder, like being put through an industrial juicer. I heard myself squeal in agony.

"Why's Joey Thumbs lookin' for you, Cole?" he rumbled in my ear. The room started to flow around me as if we were all swirling around a giant drain.

"Let him go, George," Lacy commanded, and immediately the pressure subsided.

I could actually feel blood rushing back into my arms, and my shoulder swelling like a balloon. The room was spinning and spackles of light danced in my eyes. I'd probably pass out if he groped me like that again. I tried to play it cool by reaching for my coffee with my good arm, but that smallest of motions brought me to swoon as all the energy in my body seemed to flood out of the soles of my feet. My ass headed skyward, and I crashed into the floor. I looked to the back of the room and saw Rosie, upside down, climbing out of the booth and running toward me.

Her voice came closer, heavenly and clear. "Cole? My God! Are you okay?"

"Ma'am, we have this under control," Lacy said. "We have this under control."

"You all right, Cole?" Lacy asked in a hushed voice. "For Chrissakes, George! What did you do?"

The big man shrugged, then poked me hard in the back with his foot. "What's the matter with you, huh? You in shock or somethin'?"

"I think the observation deck is a little too high," I mumbled from the floor.

"Huh? What did you say, smart guy?"

"Help him up, George," Lacy nudged. "*Gently.*"

He hefted me off the floor in one mighty pull, and my arms and legs trailed about a tenth of a second behind the rest of me—like being dragged behind a bus. My magical floating ass plopped down hard into a seat, and Rosie and Holly were immediately at my side, chattering a million miles a minute. I shook the curtains loose on my brain and straightened my eyeballs to see Rosie bearing down on Lacy Lincoln with an accusatory finger and an angry tirade about lawyers and police brutality.

"Rosie," I said to no effect, my voice wavering and weak. "*Rosie!*" I shouted.

Both women stopped mid-shouting match and stared at me as if I'd just interrupted a wedding planning. I could practically see the icy contrails their anger left in its wake, spirals of white smoke winding straight through to the back of my skull.

"I'm fine," I said, hoping that would melt the arctic stare from at least one of them. "The big man here doesn't know his own strength, caught me on my bad shoulder while he was helping me up."

McGuire stood beside me and pulled out a notepad as subterfuge, making it seem he was simply standing there taking notes while I just keeled over of my own accord. He held his pencil to his notepad as if he were about to jam it through a windpipe. As he realized that I had exonerated him of beating me down, his shoulders sank in relief, and I swear I saw a blush rise in his ham hock cheeks. I doubt it meant we were ready for sitting next to each other at a Lakers game, but he seemed less inclined to push my nose through my forehead.

"Yeah," Lacy snarled. "We were just finishing our questions. If you think of anything else, *Mister* Cole," she said, nodding to McGuire to start stomping villages on his way to the front door, "you know where to find us."

"You got it."

Lacy gave me a wink. "Be seein' ya, Cole." She tipped her platinum-on-gold head toward Rosie. "Miss Stetch."

Rose gave Lacy a hard sidelong stare, stepping under my arm to prop me up, she and Holly each taking an arm.

"Come on. Let's get you home." My two girls led me out the back through the kitchen.

Chapter 18

Whether it was a full-on blackout or just passing out from exhaustion, the next thing I knew, we were stopped in the parking lot of a run-down apartment block in Reseda. I knew it was Reseda because I could see the *Miss Donuts* sign down on Sherman Way, the one where they filmed the robbery at the end of *Boogie Nights*. That was a good fucking movie.

A door closed behind me. I let my head roll to come face to face with little Holly, staring at me through the window with sad eyes and a weak smile, nervous hands fidgeting at her sides. Then Rosie was there, shuffling her daughter out of the way and opening the door to help me out to the sidewalk.

"I'm all right," I told her as she grasped for my armpit yet again.

There were few things I hated more than feeling like I couldn't take care of myself. At the same time, I wanted her to be touching me. I needed that comfort, that connection.

Holly probably needed it too—more than anybody. Kids could be resilient and tougher than leather, but when the world closed in like a boogeyman, and all the bad things they couldn't understand piled up in their periphery and crawled over their bed at midnight, every kid just wanted to feel safe, to have someone hold them and protect them from those shadows. Holly's sad eyes spoke to that now. She needed her mother, even more than I did.

I shrugged away from Rosie and nudged her toward her baby girl. "You could have just sent me home in a cab."

Rosie looked back at me with the same sad eyes I'd seen on Holly's face. I looked away, ashamed of myself for being a prick, and when I looked back up they were a good ten paces ahead of me, Holly's arms around her mother's legs, Rosie stooping slightly to keep an arm tight around her child. I felt something... gigantic. Something I hadn't felt since Pops had died. Something good and warm and alive and right.

I wanted to be part of them, part of their lives, forever.

Then I saw it again, reflecting on the back of my brain—their faces, terrified and confused, full of pain and confusion, wood and concrete exploding all around us—and a hot electric pulse ran through my body as though I were filling with fire.

Joey Thumbs was going to pay.

Dragging *them* into this bullshit and throwing bullets their way, over a record? I wanted his blood on my hands, to tear every cell of his lousy fucking body apart. I wanted to burn him alive, and to listen to every last inch of him hiss and pop and scream for mercy. I wanted vengeance, justice for what he'd taken from that little girl. I was awash with what Pops had called our *fuochi d'ebollizione* – the boiling fire. It was good for two things, he always said: loving a woman, or killing a man.

Joey Thumbs was going to die.

"Cole, are you all right?"

The red blaze fell away at the sound of her voice. I had barely moved, while the girls were already at the top of the landing of the wide front stairs. Rose observed me carefully, probably trying to decide whether I had suffered brain damage or a total nervous breakdown.

Holly broke away and ran down the stairs toward me, hitting the sidewalk full tilt, plowing into my legs and wrapping her arms around me like a vice.

I gently removed her vice grip and dropped to my knees, half from being physically drained, half from emotional exhaustion. I pulled her back to me and held her as tight as I dared, feeling a hot razor slice of heartbreak bring tears to my eyes as I whispered into her tiny ear.

"I'm sorry. I'm so, so sorry." I said it over and over, the words falling out of me like water pouring over the edge of a teeming barrel. It wouldn't stop. An ocean of sadness and regret washed through me, pushing at the walls of my chest, ready to crack me open and flood out, and take the whole of California back into the sea.

By the time Rosie reached us, I was sobbing and this little girl—little angel—was hushing me, telling me that everything would be all right. Rosie separated us and helped me back to my feet, putting one arm around me and one around Holly, the three of us standing in the parking lot like a long-separated family in an airport concourse.

That's what they felt like: family. Family like I hadn't known since I was six years old. I burst with equal tides of remorse and relief. I don't know how long we stood there, three pilgrims at our private wailing wall, but it was long enough for a chill to creep into the air, and to turn the night into the stark, streetlight-pitted black you only saw in L.A.

I laughed and wiped at the wet spot under my raw eyes, apologizing as we walked together up the stairs and down a short hall to their apartment door. Rosie fumbled with her keys, finally opening the door and waving for me to enter. I bowed to Holly and let her run inside before holding the door for her mother, who paused to kiss me on the cheek as she passed.

The apartment, probably too small for a kid Holly's age, showcased the unmistakable detritus of a creative kid all over the place. Heaps of loose-leaf paper masterpieces littered the floor around the coffee table and sat stacked in sheaves on top of it. A box of hundreds of colored pencils weighted them down. Stuffed animals occupied the couch, and a rambling heap of DVDs surrounded the small TV stand. Framed pictures hung on the wall, collages of pictures of Holly with and without her mother, interspersed with framed watercolor paintings the kid had done of octopus monsters and squiggly humanoids and smudgy green trees. They were beautiful. She was beautiful.

I wasn't used to being surrounded by so much innocence and *good*.

I stood in the middle of the room, uncomfortable with my own presence there, afraid to touch anything. I didn't want to taint the magic of the place with my cynicism and smartass misery. Holly's childhood had been compromised enough—between her parents' problems, her lousy grandfather, being shot at, and watching a man almost die in front of her.

Rosie came back in from the kitchen and put a cup of tea down on the table in front of Holly, leaning across her for the remote control and flipping to some kids show on the TV. She laid the remote down, bent to kiss Holly on the top of the head, and then gestured me toward the kitchen.

I followed her and sat at a tiny round table in the corner, made of light wood, with a holly hobby pot full of flowers set on a square napkin in the center. It exuded a weird warmth, just like everything else in the apartment, as if the magic of this woman and her daughter had been absorbed into everything they owned.

I had a quick flash of my own mother, standing at a sink washing dishes. I was maybe five years old, coloring in a Hong Kong Phooey coloring book, a water glass full of weeds and wildflowers I'd brought her sitting in front of me on the formica table. I looked up to see her smiling at me with the sun shining through her hair like a halo.

Then it was gone, just as fast as it had appeared, and I stared at a cup of instant coffee in a ceramic mug with kittens on it, a pair of white tablets beside the cup.

"Sorry, I only had instant," Rose said from behind a cupboard door.

"I don't drink much coffee at home."

I must have looked of dumfounded and clueless when she turned back to me, still staring at the cup in front of me.

"Cole?" She set her cup of tea across from me and folded her legs beneath her as she sat down to face me. "Who was that woman at the restaurant? The detective?"

"What?"

"The woman detective. Who is she? You seemed to know her pretty well." A clear note of jealous misery attached to her question.

Somewhere in another dimension, somebody threw a couple more clowns on top of the elephant sitting on my back, and I heard the crack of one more chunk of spine. "Her name is Lacy Lincoln. She's bad news, way too serious about her job and way too free-handed in how she goes about doing it. The big guy—"

"His name was Maguire, right? I'm not worried about him," she shot back with the sharp end of her stick.

"You're not going to play the jealous girlfriend now, are you? They were cops. They wanted to throw me a beating and lock me in a cell until I could do them some good."

"She seemed to know you pretty well. Did you two ever...?"

I answered with a sigh.

"I'm sorry," she said. "It's not really fair of me to ask those kinds of questions after we've known each other for, what? Three days?"

"It's all right. It's been an eventful three days." I reached across the table and took her hand.

She bit nervously at her luscious bottom lip. "What am I doing? We were just shot at! My daughter was shot at! That poor man could die, and I'm acting like a teenage drama queen with—"

"Rosie, you've been through a lot tonight. Sometimes your brain shoves you in a certain way, to distract you while it takes care of the nasty business you don't want to know about. What's important is that you and Holly are okay."

"It was my dad, wasn't it? I mean—not that he did it—but he was the reason, right? That was because of him?"

How could I lie to her glorious face?

"Yeah, it started because of him, but those guys were after me, not you. At least, I think—"

I put my face in my hands as it occurred to me, like a slap in the face, that not only could they have actually been after Rose and Holly, but that they might still be in danger. The point may not have been to kill me, or just me. Maybe they were trying to put the pressure on

Stetch. Thumbs would want to get the record free and clear, provide for his boss and keep the money.

But how would he have known where they were going? We were followed, but not all the way to the restaurant. Someone told the triggers where to aim. Who even knew where we'd be? Menlowe? Danny? Couldn't be. I didn't even know where we were going until I was already driving the car. Stetch?

"But why?" The cup in her hand was shaking. "Why would they shoot at us? At a little girl, for chrissakes?"

"I think I know who arranged it, and he's the kind of guy who would happily mow down a nun to get to the car wash. Did you tell anyone where we were going?"

She put the cup down and stared past me at the corner of the ceiling, trying to force herself to remember.

I swallowed down the bitter, powdery brown liquid in my own cup and kept my eyes on her, waiting.

She slowly shook her head and knitted her brows over those lovely eyes, then sighed and gave me a forced smile, troubled and faraway. She was hiding something.

"My dad? Maybe? I might have mentioned we had a date at dinner last night."

"You had dinner with your dad?" She wouldn't have had time to make it to the home for mealtime after she'd dropped me off at Dingo's.

"No, with Joseph Testaverde. He wanted to talk about the record, Dad's record."

The red came back in a flood. I stumbled away from the table, knocking the chair behind me and sending the mug crashing to the floor in a hundred pieces, spilling its rusty brown innards on the linoleum.

"He was a very nice man. Very charming and polite...."

I backed into a wall, desperately fighting the urge to grab her, shake her, slap her in her stupid, beautiful face. I wanted to put my fist through something.

Rosie cowered in her chair, well aware of the foul cloud of rage and violence swirling around me.

"He... I know you said to stay away from him... he... he seemed harmless," she pleaded.

I fought through the crimson torrent rushing through my skull and tried my worst to speak clearly and calmly. I probably looked on the verge of full silverback gorilla aggression.

"Joseph Testaverde is the man who tried to kill us." The words clawed their way through a wall of clenched teeth.

Rosie's face paled and her eyes widened in abject terror at what she had done. It was a low blow to put it to her like that, to put that blame on her shoulders instead of keeping it on mine. I'd just told her that she had nearly gotten her daughter killed by machine-gun fire. I was a lousy excuse for a human being, but she was....

"How could you be so—" *Stupid.*

"I'm sorry. I know you said not to talk to him. I didn't know." Tears marked their trails down her face, fast and loose. They hit the table, a puddle of regret forming around her cup.

She was stupid, and careless, and completely out of her element. She thought it was some game—all these silly people after Daddy's ridiculous record. Now she'd endangered her own little girl, brushed lips with death, and seen how terribly serious these people were.

I always forgot that normal people didn't get stabbed and shot and worked over on a weekly basis. Normal people didn't have to watch over their shoulder for a Joey Thumbs, or listen for the sound of a bullet hitting the chamber. I felt a right miserable *coont,* as Danny would have said. I wanted to reach out to her, but I'd just welded that door shut.

"Rosie," I mumbled into the kitchen floor.

To my surprise, Rosie smiled through a few last unshed tears, sighed once, and cleared her throat without looking at me. "Why don't you take those aspirin and go have a nice hot shower. I'll find you some clothes and get Holly to bed."

She unfolded her long legs from beneath herself, got slowly to her feet, and stepped toward the living room.

"Yeah, yeah. Good idea," I mumbled. I swallowed the two capsules dry and turned to find Holly throwing her little arms around my legs again.

"G'night," I said, smiling down at her big brown eyes.

"I'm sorry about your hat. I liked your hat."

"Me too, kid."

"Good night, Mon-sum-mo," she mumbled. "Am I saying it right?"

"Close enough, *Signorina.* But next time try *Buona Notte, Mossimo.*"

"Okay. Bono snotay, Monsemmo."

"*Perfetto!*" I kissed her on the top of the head.

I looked up at Rose and asked quietly, still wrung out with shame, "Where is the bathroom?"

Chapter 19

The bathroom was small, but again, filled with signs of womankind. *Cosmopolitan* and *Vogue* mags sat on the back of the toilet, a doily thing covered the tissue box, and make-up brushes, combs, and a hair-dryer built like an elephant gun lay on the counter.

I fiddled with the knobs in the bathtub to get the water hot, fired up the shower, and stripped the bloody shirt off my aching shoulder and back.

What if Arturo the waiter had spent crumpled at my feet?

I stared at myself in the mirror. The haggard old man looking back scared me shitless. Hollow, tired eyes, black around the edges, swollen jaw, scabbed lips. I looked like the end of the line, of so many lines. So many scars and disappointments on that face. It was the face of a man twice my age, and half as smart as I always imagined myself to be. I didn't recognize him at all. I took a long look at the octopus of purple and black that reached its tentacles out from my battered shoulder, snaking up my neck and roping out around my chest and ribs. I took stock of more scars, more tattoos, more reminders of my own pointless stupidity and self-abuse. What the fuck had I been doing to myself? Who the hell was this idiot glaring at me from this bathroom mirror? I shut my eyes against it, and against him.

I dropped my pants and my boxers to the floor and stumbled over a pile of discarded Lego blocks as I stepped into the shower. I swept them aside with one foot, and then let myself plop down to the floor of the tub where the hot water buffeted my face and chest. After a minute, the heat began to dull the pain that throbbed throughout my worn-out and abused shell of a body and the steam opened my chest and cleared my head. I pushed the angry red monster into the back of my cavernous brain and tried to focus on the facts.

The shooting was undoubtedly the work of Joey Thumbs. But why follow the car if they knew where we were going? Make sure we didn't change plans? That seemed a little over-cautious and considerate of a nutjob like Thumbs. Of course, there was nothing saying the tail was his. Maybe the Yakuza keeping tabs on me? The mysterious Jorge?

Another player I had yet to meet? Maybe they were both Joey Thumbs. The hit on a schmoe like me seemed out of character for a capo like DeFrancesco. I worked all the angles, but couldn't see how it would have profited Tommy DeFrancesco, and if there was no profit, Tommy would never put his neck out like that. Maybe Tommy wanted me tailed and Joey Thumbs wanted me dead.

That made sense. Tommy ordered a tail, Joey Thumbs gave us a tail. Then he showed us the other end of the rabid tiger. A psychopath's vendetta over a few harsh words, and a little girl gets machine-gun fire whistling past her head. Joey Thumbs was the worst kind of animal. A wild animal who was capable of anything.

But if I was out of the picture, where would he get his lead on the record? He was crazy, but he wasn't stupid. If he didn't need me anymore, he must already know where the record was. That would mean he'd found the kid from the home, Jorge Ramirez.

There was only one person who could have given him those goods.

I bolted up and jumped out of the tub, almost bringing the curtain down with me, and quickly worked a towel over my body and shovelled myself back into my pants. I hit the hallway, shirtless and in bare feet, just as Rosie came around the corner holding the phone to her ear with a look of utter confusion on her face.

"Dad," she muttered. "Something's happened to my dad." She looked like she was about to collapse.

I grabbed her by the shoulders and pulled her to me, tucking her into my good shoulder as I scooped the phone from her hand. I put it to my ear to hear someone asking, "Ms. Stetch, are you there?"

"Hello," I answered. "What's happened?"

"Sir, I really can't discuss—"

"*What happened?*" I demanded again.

"Well, I'm not sure. There was some kind of attack. The police are—"

I hung up and helped Rosie to the couch in the other room, where Holly was waiting, wringing her little hands in anxiety and wondering what was wrong with her mother.

"Holly, honey, can you get your Mom a glass of water?" I asked her.

Once she was in the kitchen, I shook Rosie by the shoulders, gently, to get her attention. "Rosie!"

She looked up at me with those glorious emerald eyes, but she was still lost in there somewhere.

"*Rose!*" I shouted and shook again.

The glimmer of understanding re-entered her eyes, and I knew she was listening.

"Your father is going to be fine," I lied. "Listen to me. Are you hearing me? He's okay."

She nodded and gave me a weak smile. The full weight of the night had finally hit her right between the eyes.

I had to get them out of town, her and Holly. Regardless of whatever had happened to her father, they had to leave, and they had to leave fast.

"Rose, he's all right. They said he's going to be fine. Do you understand?"

She nodded again.

"Good. Now I need you to take Holly away from here, okay? Take her to Lego Land or something. Just get out of the city and don't let anybody know where you're going. No one. Do you understand? I'll call you in the morning and make sure you're all right."

She was moving slowly but seemed to have a handle on the gravity of the situation.

"Money. We can't afford—"

"Here," I said, thrusting the check into her hand. "You forgot to take this yesterday. Just use it. Everything will be all right. But if anybody besides me calls you or tries to find out where you are, you don't say anything, you just keep moving. Do you understand? Rose?"

"But, my dad.... We can't spend this."

"I'm going to get you the record. The money for the record, okay? Will you please just listen to me?" I pleaded. "Your dad will be fine. You need to go now. They will hurt you and they will hurt Holly. You need to move—*now*."

I helped her up and steered her down the hall, then turned to kneel in front of Holly, who was standing in the kitchen doorway.

"I know this is all a little scary, Sweetheart, but it's going to be okay. Why don't you go help your Mom get packed. I'm sending you guys to Lego Land for a couple of days, okay?"

She lunged forward and wrapped her arms around my neck in a vise grip. "You won't let them hurt us, right?" Her big eyes burned a hole straight through my chest.

"No, Sweetie, I won't let anybody hurt you. You go take care of your mommy for me. I'll take care of the rest. Maybe I can meet you down there in a couple of days and you can show me around Lego Land?"

"Promise me, Monssemmo?"

"Cross my heart, little girl," I lied as my heart cracked open one more time.

Chapter 20

I was halfway to the nursing home when I realized my phone was still off. The glowing red light of urgency started immediately, followed by a dozen dings for the dozen messages I'd missed. Menlowe left ten frantic messages warning me that Joey's goons were on the move. I also had a message from Skogerbo, relating his interrogation at the hands of Joey Thumbs and a couple of his goons. Sounded like Ollie got off easy. They trashed his place, broke a bunch of records, slapped him around a little, but didn't break any parts of him. He admitted that he told them everything he told me, which wasn't much.

I'd been dragging my ass, distracted by Danny and Rosie and my own bullshit, and people like Ollie and Jorge Ramirez were paying for it.

The last message was from Joey Thumbs himself. I fumbled with the buttons to pull up the recording, then clicked the speakerphone and dropped it on the passenger seat as I heard Joey Thumbs' crazy mania fill the car like so much echoing evil.

"Hey Cole! You fucking *mook*. You probably won't get this, because you'll be dead. On the off chance you do, I just wanted to let you know that we found the record. I'm gonna get it, Cole. I'm gonna keep the money and then I'm gonna pay you a visit, fuckface. You hear me? I'm gonna get you. Then I'm gonna find that redhead *figone* of yours and show her a real good time. Have her *ciucciami il cazzo* before I get rid of her? Then I'm gonna do that little *troia* of a daughter. What do you think about that, Cole? Maybe I'll keep you around just long enough to watch me stick it in that pretty, tiny little mouth... you fucking *arruso*! *Cocksucker*!"

I could feel my neck around my ears, my shoulders swelling with anger as the voice became angry and loud and the things he said got more terrible. All my muscles were threatening to tear through the skin as if I were the Incredible Hulk. Blood filled my ears, rushing and hissing like the deep inside of the Ocean, and my vision went blurry with the pressure. I could have blown more than one blood pressure cuff as I pressed my thumb through the buttons on the phone to turn off the voicemail. It took every ounce of sense I had left not to erase the message, turn around and head to Testaverde's hotel.

I'd never been so furious as I was hearing that message. I'd been angry enough to beat someone nearly to death, angry enough to tear the door off a moving cab, angry enough to fight—and kill—a ferocious, bloodthirsty bull shark. Vendetta is practically my middle name. He was going to pay. One way or another, that greasy fucking pig was going to pay.

I pulled up in front of the FloHo probably looking like a crazy hobo or an escaped inmate, and made the quick decision to sort myself out in the bar across the street. It was blessedly quiet and, after a quick snort of scotch at the bar, I went to the bathroom and splashed some water on my face, straightened my shirt, and made myself near-presentable as I'd been since this all started. I felt alive and full of purpose and as sure as I had ever been of my own fate. I knew my reason for being.

I was the avenging angel come to utterly destroy Testaverde.

Entering the Florence Henderson Continuing Care Center on this particular night, the first thing I noticed was the low mourning wail of the Hammond organ wafting out from the back of the main floor. Still trembling with anger, I forced myself to remain calm, to keep composed, and to keep the homicidal rage out of my eyes. Usually I would have taken the stairs to the second floor in any building, but I was working on autopilot, and the path of least resistance put me in the elevator next to a shrunken couple in matching cardigans who smiled at me through wet eyes as they held wrinkled hands.

"Here to visit a loved one, dear?" the woman asked. She had the permanent set, blue-rinse hair of her generation, but the lines of her face betrayed a happiness and contentment that was unusual in someone her age.

I wanted to hold out my fury like a newborn in my arms and show the world, but the face of this little old lady in an elevator made me swallow it whole. I smiled at her, unwilling or unable to break that lovely old face with my filthy rage.

"Yes ma'am," I replied. "Just checking up on a friend."

I nodded to them as I exited the elevator, feeling suddenly exhausted by the momentary release of the pure vengeance that had been running through my body like a freight train. I shook it off and put on my game face as I approached the desk.

The big woman behind the desk recognized me and stepped out to block my way. "Visiting hours are over, sir. Mr. Stetch is not well."

"Yeah, where was this high-level security a couple of hours ago? I know what happened. His daughter asked me to come and check in on him."

She crossed her meaty arms and stared me down with a look sharpened on a thousand belligerent men. "*You* still can't go in."

The tunnel vision of bloodthirsty madness started to fill my head again.

She obviously saw it in my eyes, because she took a step back and turned her head slightly, as if looking for an escape route or a quick path to assistance—maybe a weapon under the desk or an alarm trigger.

"I don't want any trouble, Lady, but I need to see Stetch and I need to know what happened here. His daughter and his granddaughter... you know Holly? The sweet little girl with the pigtails and the smile? They could be in danger from the same scumbags that came here. You want that on your conscience?"

The realization of what I was saying, followed by guilt, and finally fear, crept across her wide face like a dark cloud skirting a blood red moon.

"The police are already—"

Before she could finish stammering, I stomped past her into Stetch's room. She came in behind me and grabbed my arm, when I heard a familiar voice.

"It's all right, nurse. Let him in." Little Lacy Lincoln sat in a chair in the corner, quiet and shadowed by the curtain in the middle of the room. "You just keep turning up today, don't you Cole? Is this more of your collateral damage?"

The nurse let go of my arm and huffed away, swearing at me under her breath.

Lacy stood and stepped toward me with that sex-drenched swagger of hers, still wearing the low-cut shirt and tight suit pants she'd worn earlier, an ensemble that, on her, would have bedevilled the devil himself.

"Lacy," I said, trying to quiet the pulsing waves in my head. "Since when are you on little old man duty?"

"Funny. You obviously already know what happened. We figure it was Joey Thumbs, or some of his boys. You going to keep holding out on me, Cole? Are you going to clam up again and try for that accessory rap?" She sauntered closer until she was practically on me, caressing my arm and speaking in a husky whisper. "Come on, Cole, just you and little ol' me. We can talk. We're old 'friends', aren't we?"

"Yeah?" I replied. "The kind of friend who sics her pet gorilla on you? Where is ol' George? Out climbing the Empire State building again?"

She ran her hand gently across my face and down my chest.

"Oh, I don't need George to handle you, Mossimo Cole. Or are you actually stuck on that pretty redhead of yours?"

I lifted my head away and pushed her to arm's length. "Back off Lacy."

She looked up at me with a sultry pout and batted her eyes sarcastically. "You *are* stuck on that tall drink of cherry wine, aren't you, Cole? Well, I'll be damned. Never thought I'd see the day. All right, have it your way. All business. So what the fuck is Joey Thumbs doing beating up old men in a nursing home?"

She turned and stepped towards Stetch, lying in his bed, face bruised, eyes swollen shut. She pulled back the blankets so I could see his hands. Both hands were purple and three times their normal size.

"Dislocated both of his thumbs and shattered his wrists. They're going to transfer him to the general and operate in a few hours to try and put his hands back together, though they're not sure he'll make it anyways. Took a good beating to the face and a pretty decent concussion. That's a lot of abuse for a man his age. They've got him doped to the gills now."

She turned back to look me straight in the eye, this time with no vamp act and no threatening glare.

"So you tell me, Cole. Busting up old men, shooting machine guns at little girls. What in the *hell* is Joey Thumbs doing in *my* town and what does he have against you?"

All business was right. I'd never seen Lacy Lincoln so serious. Usually it was there, behind the bedroom eyes and the saucy come-ons, but I'd never seen her look so intense or so deadly. All of a sudden, she wasn't a land mine to avoid, a man-trap to side-step, or even a cop to steer clear of. She was the one person on the planet as pissed off as I was. She'd suddenly morphed into a sister-in-arms, and quite possibly the only confidante I was going to find.

"All right," I said. "You can buy me a cup of coffee."

***

Half an hour later, I'd told it the story, omitting a few minor details, like the continuing involvement of Kickerdick and Manlove, and my run in with the Yakuza. I was on my third cup of coffee and she was still sitting quiet in front of her first.

"A record?" she said with a healthy measure of disbelief. "Like... a vinyl fucking record? All this over a Sinatra record? Shooting at that little girl? The old man? The Ramirez kid?"

"Ramirez kid? Jorge Ramirez?"

She leaned back in her chair, always comfortable and always at home wherever she went—that was part of the allure of Lacy Lincoln. She stretched out her legs, picked up her cup and downed the remnants in one pull, then slammed the cup down on the tabletop and breathed a deep contemplative sigh that made her breasts heave in a way that's usually only appropriate in romance novels.

"Yeah, Jorge Ramirez. Thumbs' boys put the poor kid in the hospital for a long time. Joey Thumbs had his goons separate every one of his joints from fingertips to shoulders—both sides—broke his nose and ocular cavity, and smashed his jaw. Kid's lucky to be alive. He used to be an orderly at the hospital. We figured that's how they found Stetch."

I rolled my eyes and shook my head in disbelief. Maybe Stetch wasn't as senile as everybody thought. Clever old prick.

"Other way around. Stetch told them where to find Ramirez. Stetch thought Ramirez was the one who copped his record in the first place, and it looks like he was right. I need to talk to Ramirez."

Lacy raised an eyebrow and snickered. "To Ramirez? He won't be talking to anybody for quite a while, Cole. His jaw's wired shut and he's getting his eyeballs put back in place right about now."

"Shit. That's perfect, isn't it?" I grumbled, dropping my face into my hands.

"So what now, Cole? We bring in Thumbs and hope somebody stays alive long enough to point the finger at him? He's careful. Even that message he left you is non-descript enough for him to avoid any kind of prosecution. We've got him under surveillance but, without a witness, he's still free and clear."

"Fuck."

"You know what Sinatra would have done? I read about this one time, when some douchebag was manhandling Liza Minnelli in a hotel room. Her kid calls Frank, who's thousands of miles away in Florida. Five minutes later, ten guys show up, drag the sonofabitch out of the hotel and beat the shit out of him for laying his hands on a woman. Maybe somebody needs to take Joey Thumbs for a long walk in a short alley."

A magnificent, absolutely-fucking-brilliant idea popped into my head, fully formed and perfectly suited not only to extract a small measure of personal revenge but, hopefully, put Joey Thumbs away for a long time. If I didn't kill him first.

"What kind of surveillance?"

"What?"

"What kind of surveillance do you have on Thumbs?"

"What do you have in mind, Tiger?" she growled, turning the cougar act back on.

"Let me make a couple of calls," I replied with a smile. Yeah, I had an idea all right. "You guys still use those tasers? The real juicy ones?"

She eyed me suspiciously, but seemed firmly on board with my line of thinking. "Buffalo jumpers? No. But I know where we can get one." She smiled.

Chapter 21

It took a couple of hours to get things together. Between Manlove and Kickerdick, Danny and Lacy, I had everything put together and ready to roll by 2AM.

Thumbs kept his entourage of four personal thugs in close quarters. His suite took up half a private floor, and his boys had camped out in two rooms between the elevator and his door. They were standard-issue Vegas muscle, none too smart, fond of booze, gambling and call girls, but Thumbs was notoriously pissy about noise when he was sleeping. He had once thrown one of his own men from the balcony of the Grand Lakeview suite of the Bellagio for waking him up at 4 AM.

So they'd be playing quietly, but playing nonetheless.

Lacy's pals on the Organized Crime Task Force had the whole floor bugged, with audio in all the rooms, but only managed cameras in the main hall outside of the elevator. They also had a key to Thumbs' suite, which they were kind enough to let us borrow, so long as we didn't compromise their surveillance. The OCTF kids played fast and loose with the rules. They didn't care how they contained and regulated gangbangers and mob tough guys. They just made them disappear. This time we were playing what Danny referred to as "The Great Rock & Roll Swindle" in deference to his love for the Sex Pistols.

Danny had been tearing up the nightclub in the lobby, making nice and buying drinks for some of Thumbs' boys before the boss retired for the night. Joey Thumbs' room went silent at 1:30, so Danny was stumbling down the outer hall and banging on the doors at 2 AM on the dot. Not wanting to wake their boss, but also not wanting to offend their new rock star pal, the goombahs quickly pulled Danny into their card game, and were happy to let him order up a few bottles and some food as long as he was quiet and kept betting large.

Around 2:30, a hotel employee exited the elevators with a large room service cart. The hotel worker collected his tip, left the cart in the room and left the way he came in. Nothing out of the ordinary. Nothing except that, once the cart was in the room, just as Danny had excused himself to the *loo*, these large, well-dressed Italian-American gentlemen began to feel a little lightheaded.

Ten minutes later, when Danny stepped into the hall, he happened to be wearing a SWAT-style gas mask. He also happened to pass two gentlemen exiting the elevator. One of these gentlemen was described in reports as very large, heavily tattooed and carrying a briefcase. The second man was smaller, about the same size as the hotel worker who had delivered the room service cart, and carried what looked like a "large purple phallus." Both men wore plastic gloves.

Not too long after that, the camera mysteriously blinked out for about fifteen minutes. Strangely enough, the microphones were still in play and caught a series of noises that sounded like fabric rustling, a few heavy thuds, wet sounds like shampoo squeezed from the bottle, slapping sounds, giggling, and the clicking sounds of a camera flash.

I crept past Manlove and Kickerdick redecorating the auxiliary room, and used the key to sneak quietly into Joey Thumbs' expansive suite. Lacy's techs had also shown me the plans to the room and the location of the mics they'd planted, which I carefully disengaged before unloading the contents of my backpack and entering the bedroom. I found Joey Thumbs lying prone on his back, naked, spread-eagled with the sheets kicked off.

I stood there a long couple of minutes, staring at the rotten sonofabitch. It took every ounce of my threadbare sanity not to tear his throat out with my bare hands, or smash his skull to pulp with the heavy-looking lamp on the bedside table. He deserved to die, but that could wait. I had no doubt that, should this play out right, we would meet again... soon. I would stick to the plan, for Rosie. For Holly. I promised I'd get the record. The greater vengeance could wait. Besides, this was going to be a hell of a lot of fun, and I couldn't have asked for a better setup.

I very carefully sat at the end of the queen mattress and took aim with a small flashlight as my guide. Joey Thumbs sat bolt upright with an owl-like screech, clutching at his groin as the electrodes dug into the flesh of his exposed scrotum. I'd fired the electrodes but waited to hit the action button until he was awake. I'm sure some would say it was a sick pleasure I took in seeing Joey Testaverde writhing in pain, the hair singeing off his balls, and his hands clamped to his Johnson hard enough to turn it purple.

"Hiya Joey!" I said cheerfully once the tremor from the initial shock had subsided.

He looked at me with pure disbelief in his eyes; as if the one absolute impossibility in his universe was me sitting on his bed and shocking him in the junk with a tazer. To be fair, it probably was nearly impossible. Anger replaced the bewilderment and he reached to yank out the electrodes sunk into his tender bits.

Just to make sure I had his attention, I gave him another jolt, which made him scream out like a teenage girl in a slasher flick. It was glorious. While he was thrashing on the bed, I gave him a solid clout with the sap I'd been hiding in my back pocket. That knocked him loopy enough to twist his arms back and throw the cuffs on him, and snap them to the headboard. They were fuzzy and pink. It was all Manlove had, but they worked just fine for keeping his hands away from the tazer bullets in his crotch.

"We need to have a little chat, Joe."

"*Fuck you, fracicone!*"

He grunted, groaned, struggled against the cuffs and spat a mouthful at my feet. He was rubbing his thighs together like a snake-dancer trying to dislodge the probes.

"*Boys! Tessio! Mo? Johnny? Tessio! Boys!*"

I giggled. Honest-to-Christ, I giggled like a schoolgirl and pressed the switch again, enjoying every second of his writhing agony. When I let up the juice, he sunk back on the bed, broken and quiet.

"Now, what exactly makes you think it's okay to have your goons fire machine guns at innocent women and little girls?" I asked, pacing the width of the bed.

"Fuck you," he replied weakly. "You're a dead man."

I laughed loudly and hollered in his face to clarify his situation for him. "*Nobody is coming to save you, Joey!*"

Realization filled his beady little eyes with fear. Now he was crawling back into the headboard, as if he was hoping to get away from me by passing through the wall. Nobody was coming for poor little Joey, and now he knew it.

"Please, Cole. Come on. We can cut a deal here... Paisans, right?"

"Gee, Joe, a couple of seconds ago you were calling me *fracicone* and telling me to fuck myself. Now you want to be pals?"

I lit up the joy buzzer attached to his nuts and watched him twitch.

"I don't make deals with scumbags that beat up helpless old men or threaten to rape little girls."

"*P-P-P-P-Please!*" he yelped through the hum of the tazer.

I let go of the switch and sat down on the bed next to him, as he curled his legs up into himself and whimpered like a puppy.

"You know, Joe, All week long I've had Sinatra stuck in my head. Sinatra on the radio, Sinatra on the TV, everybody telling me stories, Sinatra this and Sinatra that...."

He reasserted himself by thrashing his legs to kick at me, feeble and ineffective after a few thousand volts.

"Sinatra wasn't shit!" Joey growled, snapping like a caged dog. "Fucking pussy from Jersey."

"That's funny, Joey. Does Tommy D like that one?"

He hoarked up a nasty glob of phlegm and rifled it through his teeth at me. I dodged the spittle and smiled wide. It was so damned satisfying having him trapped and neutered, the big bad bogeyman so helpless.

"You know that part in *The Godfather*? The part with the horse head?" I rambled, taking my time and feeling relaxed and in control. "What am I saying? Of course you do. Your whole life is one bad Pacino impression, isn't it, Joe?"

He lay there, seething, but not daring to push my trigger-finger. He was probably already daydreaming about the things he'd do to my poor metacarpals once he got his hands free.

"That scene, the one with the horse head in the bed, that was based on a true story. Frank was having a hard time getting back into pictures, so Sam Giancana had some boys pay a visit to Harry Cohn at Columbia pictures, and *convinced* him to give Sinatra the part."

Thumbs stayed perfectly still in the center of the bed, but his eyes were lit up like firecrackers.

"So what? You got a point, fucko?"

I couldn't help smirking as my thumb slowly hovered over the button.

His face immediately shifted back to abject fear, tears welling up in his eyes.

"The point, Joe, is that it pays to have friends. Right now, you have none."

I stood and glared down at him, asserting my dominance and keeping as much distance between me and the smell of burning hair as I could.

"Here's what we're going to do, Joey," I said quietly. "First, you're going to speak very clearly into this recorder and admit that you sent those guys to shoot at us. You're going to admit to beating up Stetch and Jorge Ramirez, and anything else that pops into your pea-sized brain. Then you're going to tell me where the record is. *A capisce, paisan?*"

He mumbled something from the crook of his arm and wiped his face on the pillow.

"What was that, Joe? You'd rather I fried your balls off? Okay."

"*Fine!*" He looked defiantly into my face with cold hard eyes, and then wavered as he caught the movement of my thumb over the trigger. "Fine. I said that would be fine. I'll do what you want."

Twenty minutes and two tries later—I had to make sure he didn't mention my little... enticement—I had his full confession, the name of the town in Mexico where Jorge Ramirez had sent the record to his Aunt Maria, and the keys to Joey's Jaguar. I left Joey on the bed, but made sure that he was conscious enough to enjoy taking part in Kickerdick and Manlove's little photo shoot taking place in the adjoining room. When they were finished, they'd quietly disappear.

I handed Joseph Testaverde's full confession over to Lacy Lincoln and the OCTF. *Everybody wins.* Well, everybody but Joey Thumbs and his sorely abused nether-regions.

Lacy promised me they'd bag him as soon as he tried to leave the hotel, and keep him for at least twenty-four hours.

That gave me time to get to Durango, and kept Thumbs preoccupied and, hopefully, away from Holly and Rosie, who would be halfway to Lego Land by now. He'd be loose and looking for payback soon enough, but I had a record to find and my first good lead to follow. I also had a nice new Jaguar to do it in.

Chapter 22

Durango. According to Joey Thumbs and his electric magic 8-balls, Jorge Ramirez had sent the hot Sinatra to his aunt on a ranch in Durango, Mexico. An intensive half-hour of info-relay and double-entendre with Lacy Lincoln, and I had found out that it was actually a massive estate just outside of Gómez Palacio. It belonged to a family by the name of Ramirez, a wealthy, and notorious, family of successful drug dealers who managed the largest Marijuana grow-op in the southwest.

Perfect. Just what I needed: one more racially-based organized crime family. It probably wouldn't help that, based on the name, this was also a family affair. All evidence pointed to these drug smugglers being the surviving relations of the original owner of the record, the late Georgie Ramone.

Lacy had told me that her sources with the D.E.A. had been keeping tabs on Jorge Ramirez. He was a favored nephew, sent to L.A. a few times a year to distribute the Ramirez product, which also made him the natural choice to entrust with locating and "retrieving" the Sinatra from Obie Stetch. The only question was why. Why risk the nephew, let alone the family business, for a record?

That same question kept popping up with all the interested parties.

Why would the Yakuza offer a cool million for it? Why would the mob shoot at little girls? I could understand the appeal of owning a piece of history like that, but what cost was too high? I couldn't even fathom the first offer of fifty grand from DeFrancesco. It was a record— just a flat, black hunk of vinyl with grooves scratched into it. I knew what it meant to men like Tommy D and Takahashi Kenzo. To them it was status and control. What was it to this Mexican drug cartel? What was I really chasing out here in the desert?

Wheels spun in my head, doing what they always did, whether I liked it or not. The back of my brain was operating hot, spinning the permutations of the problem, seeking out the possible outcomes and looking for just the right angle—the one where Rosie and Holly came out the winners, and I lived a long, lovely life with them, playing trumpet and paying my bills without getting my ass kicked.

Seemed like a long shot at best.

It was a long-haul drive into Durango province, which, although mostly mountains and forest, was still hot as hell. The cush leather seats, tinted windows and superior A/C in Joey Thumbs' Jaguar sure took the sting out of it. It almost made it too. I was only about an hour from Gómez Palacio when the car died.

The wind had kicked up a sandstorm out of nowhere and I couldn't really see if I was still on the road. The rattling, bucking and high whine of the engine probably should have tipped me off, but I wasn't overly concerned with the state of Joey's fancy ride. I should have been. The wind ceased it's mad howling as fast as it had roared out of the dunes in the first place and, when I stepped out into the full blast daylight to check the engine, I was almost crushed to a fine powder under the weight of the afternoon sun and complete lack of air flow. It was like Death out there — sill, silent, and hot as the inside of a nuclear meltdown.

I trudged to the front of the car and jammed my hands under the hood to find the release clasp, only to find my fingertips seared to the metal with a startling, bone-aching burn that almost immediately began to throb unbearably. I cursed, kicked the fender with an overheated foot and fell back on my ass. I pulled off my jacket and wrapped it around my hands before I dug under the hood again and found the latch. More oppressive heat blasted out into my face as I lifted the hood to find a solid layer of sand covering every part of the engine. It smelled like scorched tires and burning oil and was hot enough to induce a profound light-headedness.

I was screwed.

I gathered what meager supplies I had in the car — flashlight, map, a couple of bottles of water, and three leftover tacos from a stand in Juahaca a couple of hours back. I found a blanket and some road flares in the trunk, along with a 9mm Glock, a roll of bills that would choke Linda Lovelace, and a shotgun with plenty of the requisite ammo. I wrapped everything up in the blanket and tied it up like a hobo from an old cartoon, tying it through the trigger-guard of the shotgun — after emptying the shells, of course — and slung my makeshift pack over my shoulder. I tucked the pistol into my waistband, jammed the cash into my pocket, and wrapped my jacket around my head like an Egyptian camel salesman.

Then I started walking.

I made good for an hour or so, despite burning red arms and sweat pouring down my grime-covered face. I was never happier to be wearing my old motorcycle boots, because the only part of my body that wasn't completely raw with sand was my feet, which I'm sure would have been bloody nubs in any other kind of footwear. Now I knew how Clint Eastwood was supposed to feel when he stumbled out of the desert in those old gunslinger movies, all cracked lips and sandblasted leather face.

I was starving and my blood sugar was bottoming out, and soon I was barely moving. The tacos had turned into a hot mush of questionable meat, brown lettuce and a seriously unpleasant melange of sour cream and guacamole, but I ate them anyways, gagging down the worst parts with one of the bottles of water, while I sat on a big sandstone rock at the side of the road.

A truck drove past and, seeing a grimy, mad-looking *guero*, drove on without slowing, despite my manic waving and shouting with my mouth full of spoiled taco mush. A couple of other trucks passed me as I walked, both slowing just enough for the men in the cab or up in the truck bed to stare and chuckle to themselves as they drove on.

One man barked, "Hey! *Pendejo*! You're going to shoot your own balls off like that. *Estupido*!"

Their collective laughter faded into the distance with them, and I was still slowly stumping along the side of the road when the taco-sickness struck. Everything from my testicles up squeezed hard into my panicked guts and retched forward, trying to escape my esophagus. I hit the sand hard on all fours, and quaked violently as a stream of putrescent brown and green shot out of me and painted the desert in a streak of vomit. My final stores of energy went with it, and I could barely will myself to stay on my knees, let alone try to force my withered body to stand and walk another step.

Whether it was a combination of the heat, the lack of sleep, and the violent spasms racking my body, or entirely because of the food poison swirling through my veins, things began to spin. The azure blue of the sky met the blinding white heat of the sun and merged with the twinkling sand. It spiralled out of control around me, as if I were caught at the bottom of a fierce whirlpool pushing me through the floor of my own consciousness until I felt like a bug mashed under the toe of a heavy boot. Weak and devoid of any will to move, I collapsed and let exhaustion and sickness fade into the back of my eyelids as sleep took me.

"Hey. *Hola, Señor.. ¿Es usted enfermo? Señor?*"

"*Javier! Venga ayudarme a levantar a este hombre!*"

"*Sí, papa*"

"*¡Uno... dos... tres!*"

I woke with a screech as my torn shoulder bounced off the inside of a truck bed. Two dark Mexicans were staring at me from the open tailgate. The older one wore a huge black moustache and a filthy white-straw hat. The young one was a head taller with thickly muscled arms dangling from the shoulders of a torn t-shirt that said, "Hammer Don't Hurt Em," in unmistakable early 90s text. They were both dirty and dripping with sweat. The truck bed smelled like a goddamn goat farm, which did not help my nausea or my headache.

I winced as the sun caught my eyes.

"You okay, mister?" the younger one asked in a rough Spanglish.

"Yeah." I shielded my eyes and coughed out a clot of dust. "Yeah. Bad tacos."

They laughed and muttered between them. The only things I caught for sure were *Americano* and *estupido*, and I was surely that.

"Do you need a ride somewhere, gringo?" asked the older one.

I had partially regained my bearings, and crawled up to sit on the tailgate in front of them. I noticed the younger man had a water bottle in his hand.

"*Por favor?*" I asked, gesturing to the bottle.

He handed it to me and watched with curiosity as I drained half the bottle down my raw gullet.

"*Gracias.*"

He waved me off as I tried to hand the bottle back, so I swallowed the rest, saving just enough in my mouth to swish and spit the foul vomit and rancid meat flavour from my mouth.

"I'm trying to get to the Ramirez estate. Near Gómez Palacio?"

Right about then I remembered the gunny sack and the shotgun. I'd no sooner glanced down to see it laying by the now dried stain I'd passed out in, than the kid spotted my glance and turned to pick it up. I jumped to get there first, and came nose-to-nose with an ancient colt revolver that the old man jabbed into my face. I sat back and held my hands up as he reached out and pulled the Glock from my waistband.

"Let's just take it easy, okay? What are you guys, a couple of banditos? You want my shotgun? Take it. All yours."

They laughed. The old man took the gun out of my face and jammed it into my ribs instead. "What you want with Estado del Ramirez? Eh, gringo?"

"I have some news about a man named Jorge Ramirez. Want to talk to whoever is in charge."

"Well, you are in luck, hombre. We will take you there, right now."

"Thanks?"

The kid stepped up beside the old man and racked the shotgun, levelling it at my head. "First you give us your money, *pendejo*."

I shrugged and dug Joey Thumbs bankroll out of my pocket. It wasn't my money anyways, so let em' have it. "Can I get those bottles of water back?"

The old man laughed and nodded to the younger one, who threw the water at me as he lifted the tailgate closed.

I quickly unscrewed the cap and began to guzzle down the water, which was now hot and stale, but still wet and soothing. I'd almost drunk my fill when a taut, wiry arm pulled me down by my throat until I was trapped, strangling against the side of the truck-box. I panicked and went into a blind rage as something punched through the side of my neck and hot blood trickled down my throat. The animal fury dropped away in a wave of sudden comfort. My last thought was what a lousy place it was to die, waylaid by a couple of dirty banditos in a shitty truck in the hot, miserable fucking desert. The pressure lifted from my throat and chest, and I slumped like a rag doll into the bottom of the truck bed.

Another tide of exhausted contentment washed over me, and I stared in bemused wonder at the sprigs of rotten straw in front of my face. Then the world went black one more time.

Chapter 23

Bees were buzzing through my ears, back and forth through the cavernous center of my skull. At least, that's what it felt like—a low droning hum behind my eyes and filling the air. My mouth was dry, and itchy as hell, but when I reached to scratch, I found my arms were quite inconveniently tied to the chair I was sitting in. My legs were likewise encumbered, and I looked down and came face-to-face with my old friend, Mr. Johnson. I didn't remember stripping down and tying myself to a chair, but here I was nonetheless.

As I slowly rolled my head around on a weak neck trying to survey my surroundings, my head began to clear and started getting back to its job. Vague images floated in the back of my mind—a green river snaking through the sand, a dirty hunk of straw, an old man and a kid laughing, the taste of sick and beef, a stinging jab to the neck. The last made me jump and instinctively throw my head to one side to protect the tender spot. Now I remembered. Like a fucking idiot. Rotten tacos. And the two swarthy gents in the shitty old truck.

I'd seen enough old detective flicks to know I'd been drugged, stuck with a questionable needle right in the goddamn jugular. But why? And who the hell drives around with a syringe full of knock-out juice? The first order of business was to get out of the damn chair and find some clothes.

I squeezed my eyes shut tight and willed them to behave. Clearer eyes checked the room again, but it was just an old wine cellar with a lot of dusty bottles, and a single window dug out of the clay wall on the opposite side of the room. Whispers of dust danced in pale sunbeams that fell in perfect lines from that window. It looked just big enough for me to fit through if I could get out of the damn chair. My first thought was to bounce my way to one of the wine shelves, try to break a bottle and then hope I could hold on to a piece of glass and cut myself loose, which was an accumulated shitload of *if*.

As I got my legs under me and rocked forward to try for a jump, I got all caught up and rolled forward over my knees, and ended up beating the dirt out of the floor with my face.

Presumably because of all the noise I was making, thrashing around and moaning in pain on the floor, a door opened to my left. I struggled and twisted and managed to scrape my face across the floor underneath all the weight of my body, and turned my head to look at a pair of well-kept snakeskin boots. They stopped mere inches from my nose, and then a face appeared, upside-down—a dark, handsome face, like Valentino, with a thin moustache and slick hair. Even upside-down I recognized Jorge Ramone, or at least the spitting image of Georgie in his prime.

I was beginning to see the sailboat behind the mess of crazy squiggles. My head was clearing and synapses firing. A very strange story was coming together. Very strange indeed.

"You are Mossimo Cole, no?" the face asked.

"Yeah," I replied from under my own ass. "Little help?"

The chair was rocked back to its full, upright position, and I twisted at the last second to avoid sitting on my own nuts.

"Thanks." I shook the dizzy fog out of my head. "Though you seem to have me at a loss here. I mean, I'm sitting here bare-ass naked, tied to a chair, and have no fucking clue where I am or who the hell you are. Where are my clothes?"

"I am the man asking the questions, Mossimo Cole."

He was trying to play bad cop, but I didn't think he really had the temperament.

"Your clothes are being washed, as you have been. You made quite a mess of yourself, Señor. You were very ill. The bonds are merely a precaution until I understand why you have come to Estado del Ramirez."

Now he was the good cop? This would be easier than I thought. The guy was working from the TV cliché handbook, and was not a good actor. I just needed to know how far I could push.

"Why should I say anything to someone who obviously kidnapped me from the middle of the goddamn desert?"

I feigned indignation, hoping to suggest my innocence as well as gauge the man's temper and intent. If he started beating the hell out of me, I was in trouble. If he stayed calm and polite, or put on false bravado, I could probably talk my way out of the chair, if not the situation.

"*Let me out of here! Help!*" I bellowed, thrashing against the chair.

"Tell me who sent you!" he demanded.

"*Untie me!*" I hollered in his face.

"Please, tell me why you are here." He came back like a mouse facing an elephant.

"Let me the fuck loose!"

"Please, Señor Cole, calm down. Let us talk peacefully."

I had him. He was no gangster. That's not to say I was free and clear, but it certainly opened the window a crack wider. Now was the time to make my play.

I smiled up at him with the sly look of the man holding the ace. I made my mad, scrambling bet, but I did it with moxie, like Sinatra would have done. No fear, baby. No doubt. *"Estoy buscando a su madre."*

"Mi madre?"

"Mary? Red hair, long legs, looks like Rita Hayworth?"

"What do you know about my mother, gringo? You shut your mouth before I...."

He stepped towards me as if he thought he should defend her honor, but unsure of exactly what he was defending it from, or whether he'd get slapped for it. He was like a puppy that had been smacked in the nose but didn't understand why.

Before I could show him, we were interrupted by the sound of heels clicking down the steps and onto the dusty floor.

"It's all right, Darling," came a soft voice with just a hint of the wavers of age.

She stood behind him, silhouetted by the light from the doorway — smaller, greyer, but still beautiful, even in her seventies. There was no mistaking those genes. This was Mary Stetch.

"Why are you looking for me, Mr. Cole? Did Obadiah Stetch send you here?"

Now I was embarrassed, sitting balls-out in front of a septuagenarian drug-kingpin grandma. Especially one that still looked better than most forty-year-olds.

"Can I get some pants? A blanket or something?"

"I have seen a penis before, Mr. Cole," she said with no small measure of mockery. "Why are you here? Before I'm forced to do something you will most certainly regret."

I swallowed my pride and tried to ignore the breeze on my twig and berries. "Mary Stetch? Or Ramone?"

"Ramirez, actually. Now get to the point."

It struck me like the end of a shitty movie. The twist was obvious, but it rolled right past you while you sat there wondering why you were watching at all. The Ramirez kid didn't use a fake name. He was named for his uncle. Jorge *Ramone* was the stage name.

"Long story short? I'm here for the Sinatra record. The one that your nephew almost got himself killed to get to you. There are some very bad men involved who want that piece of vinyl, and they'll stop at nothing to get it, including shooting at your five-year-old great-granddaughter."

I waited for it to sink in and register on her face. I wasn't sure that she knew about Holly, but she had to know about Rosie. I wanted to test the waters and see if she was going to show some concern for the granddaughter she'd never bothered with.

Mary stared me into the chair with incredulous eyes. "What are you talking about, Mr. Cole? Is this some kind of trick? Some sick joke Obadiah has sent you to play on me?"

Fury rose in her face and in the taut muscles of her arms and legs. She stood shaking for a single second, then moved in a blur of motion.

Her hot breath on my face was nothing compared to the rather cool blade of a knife laid upside of my Johnson. Maybe I'd slightly misjudged how much she knew.

She held my throat tight with one hand and tapped the blade against my member with the other. Her deep, velvet whisper of a voice dripped with vitriol. She shook with anger and her grip was like a vice around my airway. I choked and twisted, but she held me with an unnatural strength.

"I am going to cut this thing off and send it to Obadiah Stetch in a gift-wrapped box. My daughter died in 1974, you bastard! He killed her! He kept her from me and then he killed her! I haven't spoken to that sonofabitch in more than thirty years, but so help me God, I will kill him dead if I ever see him again!"

"Well if you had," I croaked out, "you'd know that your daughter had a baby girl named Rose before she killed herself."

It was a risky gamble, bringing up the suicide angle. It could have enraged her further and resulted in the filleting of my most treasured body part. Thankfully, it had the opposite, and intended, effect of stopping her in her tracks. She eased off with the knife, which was no small relief. I felt my balls loosen underneath me, and took a deep swallow of air as she released her grip on my windpipe. Now I knew she'd protect Rosie and Holly. Now I knew I could trust her with the girls I loved.

"And why should I believe some hired detective?" She stood tall and defiant in front of me, an awe-inspiring woman.

I could have easily kept stringing her along, but there was no point. Where Junior was a reluctant hoodlum at best, Mama Ramirez was the real deal. Time to give up the goods.

"If your boys still have my phone, there's a picture."

She nodded Junior towards the door, and he came back seconds later with my phone and what looked like my pants, but clean and folded like they were brand new from the Old Navy. He set them near me on the floor, and handed his mother the phone.

"Why are you giving it to *me*?" she asked, standing rigid and cool. "I don't know how to use those damn things. *Untie* him."

She maintained her guard until she was sure I wasn't playing games. I had to respect that. She may have been a drug maven and a quick-draw with a blade, but she was shrewd and possessed an innate... 'nobility' that immediately set her apart.

Pops had that—that thing that makes people want to follow a great leader.

Junior pulled a pearl-handled switchblade from his pocket and sprung the business end with a deadly sounding *snikt*.

"Birthday present?" I asked.

He smiled weakly and stepped behind me to slice the ropes around my hands, and then my feet.

I took a quick second to rub some life back into my wrists. I eyeballed my pants, but seeing the look of supreme impatience on the face of my host, I decided it would be best to show her the picture first. It would also show her that I didn't have anything to hide, although the places I could feasibly hide something at the moment were terribly minimal.

"I don't know what you think a picture will prove, Mr. Cole."

I took the phone and clicked a few buttons to get to the right place, then flipped back through a few pictures to find one I had taken at Babalu, before the bullets started flying. It was a picture of the three of us—Rosie, Holly and me—huddled together under the watchful eye of my camera phone. There was no mistaking the bloodline in their faces, and it showed that I wasn't just some jerkoff working for the old man.

I handed her the phone and watched the ice melt and the air warm around her. I quickly struggled into my pants, and was fastening the last button when she wavered as if she would faint. I jumped to reach out and steady her, grabbing her shoulders to help her regain her footing, and she laid her hand on top of mine. This time her touch was surprisingly gentle.

"My god." She wept into her hand. "How is this possible?"

"I'm not here for Obie Stetch, Mrs. Ramirez. I'm here for *them*. I love them and I need your help to protect them."

It was the first time I'd said it out loud, or even admitted it to myself, and it brought a wet knot to the middle of my chest. I found myself praying in the back of my mind, as if by instinct, that they were all right.

Small pools collected in the corners of Mary's eyes, threatening to spill over the tiny wrinkles of her face like an alluvial flow. She still held one thin, elegant hand against her mouth—a fascinating reaction. She registered my curious stare by immediately straightening her posture and clearing her throat, an almost instantaneous return of composure.

"I believe we need to speak thoroughly of this problem, Mr. Cole. Jorge will take you to your things and I will await you in my study."

She turned abruptly, probably as much to cover her emotions as to affect her importance, and stepped gracefully out of the room.

"Is she always this warm?" I asked Junior while fastening my belt.

"Mi Madre is a great woman, but she has been through hell in her long life, and she has seen much that should never be seen."

"Ok then," I said, stifling a grin. "Take me to my socks."

Chapter 24

"Drink, Mr. Cole?" Mary Ramirez stood at a bar cart with her back to me when I entered the room.

It was the kind of study you see in old movies, all rich, dark wood, and expensive furniture with tacked upholstery. Philip Marlowe would have loved it. Framed paintings by Degas and Picasso tastefully adorned the walls, and the desk looked like someone had carved it from a single redwood. Light spilled in through thick velvet curtains and fell in tight beams on the polished hardwood floor. It was elegance and power made into a room.

"Got any coffee?" I asked.

"Of course. I'll ring Jorge to bring some, if you're sure you wouldn't prefer something harder."

She stepped to the desk and sat in a high-backed chair with what looked like red velvet cushions. It was as big as a damn throne, which surely was the point. I sat in a comfortable but obviously less ornate number that easily reduced my stature so that she was peering down at me over the expanse of the desktop. She lifted an antique-looking brass telephone receiver and pressed a button as she set her crystal tumbler of scotch in front of her on the blotter.

"Yes. Bring Mr. Cole some coffee, please. What? It doesn't matter. No, it doesn't...." She turned to me with a look of exasperation that she immediately subdued in favor of her mannered hostess persona.

"Is there a particular type of coffee you would like? My son is something of an enthusiast when it comes to his coffee. Spanish? Espresso? Turkish perhaps? I'm sure you're probably used to oily truck stop blends."

I shrugged off the passive-aggressive insult and put on my best *courteous guest* face. "Actually, I'm something of an enthusiast, myself. A nice latte, with a sprinkle of cinnamon would be delightful, thank you."

"Hmmph!"

It elicited the response I was looking for, letting her know I wasn't going to kowtow simply because she appeared to be of a higher caste than a mere private investigator. We'd played enough games already, and things were sure to become deadly serious soon enough. It wouldn't take Joey Thumbs long to get himself out of whatever predicament he'd found himself in. Then he'd be gunning for me, and he knew exactly where to look.

Mary relayed my order, hung up the phone, and took a long pull of liquor before picking up my phone from the desk and staring at the picture again.

"What makes you think that these girls are related to me, Mr. Cole?" She said it with the same measured cool she had used on me in the wine cellar, and I was getting tired of it, fast.

"Can we quit playing games here?' I asked her point-blank. 'This is obviously your family. I couldn't figure it out at first. Stetch raised Rose to believe she was his one and only daughter. She only has the sneaking suspicion that he's been lying to her. Obviously, the timeframe didn't match up, what with you 'dying' in '48, right?"

"I tried to leave Obadiah many times. He threatened to have me killed, or to take my daughter away. He even threatened her life on a few occasions. When I found out what had been done to Georgie, I couldn't take it anymore. I set out to find his body in San Bruno, and to lie down beside him and die. What I found, after several days, was a shell of a man, still alive, but broken, beaten and barely breathing. I brought him here to his family. They healed him and helped me escape that foul bastard."

"And you stayed here and lived your new life. New kids, new husband, new world, right? Fake your death, forget the old kid and the abusive prick you left her with?"

I made it purposefully harsh. I wanted her to feel something, anything resembling a human emotion, and break that facade.

"No, Mr. Cole. Stetch faked my death for the insurance money, and to save his own reputation, however foul. A dead woman with no identification had quite a hard time of it back then. I tried many times to see my daughter. She was always surrounded by bodyguards and goons. Then he locked Lily up like a prisoner and threatened to kill her if I ever saw her again. He told her I had left her, that I didn't want to be her mother."

And there we had it. The dam burst and the ice queen melted. She let her glass drop to the table with a clatter as she put her hands to her face to cover her tears. She was racked with sobs and weeping when Junior came in with my latte. She must have trained him well, because he didn't look directly at her, or register his concern, other than to ask her, in Spanish, if she was all right.

"*Si, si, querido. Pesadillas del pasado. Estoy bien.*" She waved him away. *Nightmares of the past*—that was definitely one way to put it.

Junior seemed to get it. He put the coffee on the desk in front of me and turned to me with a smile, dutifully distracting me while his mother composed herself.

"It is nice to meet someone who appreciates el café, Señor Cole." He bowed slightly and left the room, glancing back to assure himself that his mother was back in control, and closed the door behind him.

"Mrs. Ramirez. Mary, I didn't mean to cause you any pain by bringing up your daughter. I just need to know what is actually going on here. As I said, I dug up a certain amount of information, but Stetch denied everything."

"He would, that rotten piece of sewer filth! Do you know how he killed her?"

"What I found says she killed herself, the same way you were reported to have died, falling off the cliffs outside of Stetch's mansion into the ocean." I hadn't told Rosie that, though she probably already knew. I shook my head in disgust. "How could he push his own daughter to that?"

"She wasn't his daughter," she stated calmly. "She was revenge. She was the knife he could forever twist in my back. She knew it, too, and tried to run as soon as she was old enough to understand. He started forcing drugs on her to keep her under control. First, he plied her with prescription drugs from the doctors he paid off. Then he just started giving her pills he bought from his Hollywood pushers. She tried to get away from him, but he drugged her more and more. She had a secret boyfriend, a musician in Obadiah's employ, and he gave her more drugs."

"Tommy Hilton. He died of a heroin overdose a few months after your daughter died. How do you know all of this if Stetch kept you away?"

"I still had friends, Mr. Cole. Many people knew I was still alive and were trying to keep an eye on Lily for me, giving her messages for me, trying to help us escape Obadiah Stetch. Eventually he sniffed them out and shut her away from everyone. He locked her in that godforsaken house and she retaliated by throwing herself into the sea, the only escape she had. He did so much to strangle and stifle and hurt that little girl. I'll never forgive myself."

She began to cry again.

I sat silent for a moment, reflecting on my own childhood terrors and the things I'd seen. Then I stood and went to her, and knelt beside her chair. I put my arms around her, and she buried her head in my shoulder and cried out for her own lost little girl. My heart broke as I understood her cold fury.

"This is why I need your help," I whispered into her ear. "Help me save these girls."

She heaved in my arms and held me close to her for a second, then pulled away and wiped her face with a handkerchief from her hip pocket as she half-laughed, half-sobbed.

I stood and picked up my phone from the desk. "Mary, I understand why you wanted the record. It was a piece of your lost lover that was in the hands of your worst enemy. I get that. But why now?"

"It's ridiculous, really. My husband, my Georgie, died just over a year ago. I was looking at photographs and mourning the man I loved. I came across a picture of him with Sinatra, a picture from that very night. I had that record made for *him*, not for Obadiah Stetch. When Obadiah found out what I had done, he went crazy. That's what led to him trying to murder Georgie. It wasn't that his wife was screwing around. It wasn't that Georgie was a better man, more talented or more handsome. It was that he had something of value. Obadiah hadn't thought to record that night at the Mozambique. To him, Sinatra was a falling star, a soon-to-be-nobody. But when Ella Fitzgerald took the stage with him, magic happened. People all over town were talking about it and, within a week, there were offers in the hundreds of dollars for a recording of that performance. When Obadiah discovered that I had paid the sound man to record it and pressed just one copy—just one—he was in greedy ecstasy."

"Then he found out who you gave it to?" I ventured.

"When he found out that I gave it to a Mexican trumpet player, he went psychopathic. He beat me, Mr. Cole. He beat me until I couldn't stand. Then he sent his goons to get the record and eliminate the *dirty beaner* who was *fucking* his wife."

I winced at the word. She trembled as it left her lips, like a rancid piece of meat, and I had a sudden wave of nauseous *déjà vu* run over my spine—Stetch's voice ringing in my ears.

"I ran," she continued. "I took Lily and we ran. He found us the very next day and took her away from me. He threatened my life and left me, beaten and alone. One of Obadiah's men was left behind to *deal with me*. Instead, he offered to tell me where Georgie was. He tried to use me like a whore and when I refused, he hit me, then laughed as he told me how they had murdered Jorge and left him in the mountains."

"But he wasn't dead."

"No. I escaped, and ran again to find him in the mountains, beaten nearly to death, his hands crushed, his face smashed to oblivion. They had broken both of his legs so that he would be sure to die there. But I found him, Mr. Cole. I found him and saved him. That bastard Stetch took my life and he took my child, but I saved my Georgie." She cried, a wide smile breaking her stone façade for a moment.

"It took five years for the doctors to repair what they had done to him. It took ten more for Georgie to pick up his trumpet again. He loved that trumpet. He could have been as great as Dizzy Gillespie or Miles Davis or any of the others, but he was never able to play properly after what they did to him... and he lived every day blaming himself for what happened to our Lily. *That*, Mister Cole, is why I took *my* record back from that evil little man. He had taken so much from so many."

Her eyes filled with fire as she finished the story, and every word of it echoed in my gut.

"Obadiah Stetch has killed, or tried to kill, every thing I have ever loved, Mr. Cole. There aren't words enough to describe how I loathe that man's very existence. So you understand my reticence to speak to you at first, but this... these girls.... Is it true? How could this be true?"

I smiled then, a tender, heart-felt smile. I liked this woman. I liked her a lot. This is what I wish my mother had lived to be, what I imagined my grandmother must have been like to tame a man like Pops.

I nodded. "It's true. Now I'm sure of it. Lily gave birth to Rose shortly before she died. Rose was raised by a series of Nannies and teachers. Stetch was a completely absent father as far as she was concerned, but I dare say, she's got your fire, Mary."

"Then she must realize what kind of monster he is."

"You have to remember, Stetch pulled the same shit on her that he put your Lily through. She thinks her mother died when she was a child, which I guess is the only true part of it, and Stetch has been the only family she's ever known. She still has a certain amount of allegiance to him, if not a curious affection. But she's your granddaughter, to be sure, and that beautiful little girl is your great-granddaughter. The problem, Mary, is that when that record went missing and old, senile Obie Stetch sent up the search flares, people came looking for it. Serious people. People who would hurt Rosie and Holly, or come here and kill every last living thing in their path, to get that record."

"We have defences of our own, Mr. Cole. We aren't exactly growing tulips in those fields."

"Some of those people are definitely on their way here by now."

"The gangster that beat up my nephew?"

"Yes. Joey Thumbs. He almost killed us last night. Beat up Stetch in his hospital room, too. Almost killed him."

"I'll have to thank him to do a better job next time."

"Do you have the record?'

She nodded to the wall behind me.

I turned and, like a goddamn Holy Grail, there it hung in its frame in the middle of the wall, individually lit, and flanked by black and white pictures. There was also a beautifully maintained horn — his horn, the trumpet that played with Sinatra. I felt a tingle in my tangle. What I wouldn't give for twenty minutes alone with that beauty. The rushing barrage of feet in the hallway, paired with the sirens, forced my eyes back to the record and my brain back to the business at hand.

"How attached are you to that record, Mary?"

"Not enough to see those girls hurt."

"Good. That's part one."

I would have explained the rest of the plan, but we were interrupted by what sounded like air raid sirens, blaring from all directions. I threw my hands over my ears and looked quizzically at Mary Stetch.

She stood from her desk, opened a drawer and stepped out brandishing a pair of silver Colt .45s.

"It would seem that your friend Mr. Thumbs has arrived."

Chapter 25

We stepped out into the warm afternoon sun, Mary Stetch and I, to the scrambled action of some thirty or forty men running out from the fields behind us, all of them brandishing large guns — shotguns, machine guns, all manner of pistols tucked into belts. They fell forward in a line in front of us like a well-trained cavalry. Pickup trucks roared in behind us in the dust, some of them laden with what looked like helicopter guns from some Oliver Stone Vietnam flick. In front of the assembled army beyond the gate, Joey Thumbs stood casually in front of three matching black sedans, dressed in a black suit, and visibly sweating like the pig he was.

"Hey Cole!" he hollered as if we were old pals.

"Thumbs," I yelled back. "How'd your party turn out last night?"

"Yeah, real funny, *fracicone*. Took me a while to convince Mr. DeFrancesco that you set that all up."

"I'll bet Tommy thought it was hilarious. He has a much better sense of humor than you. Hey! *Stugatz!* Why don't you take your boyfriends and fuck off? Looks like you're outgunned."

Mary gave me a sideways look of surprise. I shrugged and smiled.

"You may have a lot of guns, *arruso*, but I got your special fuckin' lady friends!" He turned and shouted to a giant in a black suit and shades. "*Bring em out!*"

One of the car doors opened and two figures were shoved towards the gate, one tall and topped with flame-red hair, the other tiny and fragile-looking next to Thumbs and his goons.

He had Rosie and Holly.

My stomach sank into my feet and my heart began to pound in my chest. I was about to scream out for them when a calm, powerful voice erupted from beside me.

"I don't know who you think you are, young man, but if you've hurt either of those young ladies you will answer to every single bullet in this compound!" Mary Ramirez stomped toward the gate with her guns at her side and barked an order to open the door as she approached.

I tried to warn her off, but it was too late. I ran after her and threw myself at Joey Thumbs as the gate swung wide and he raised his gun-hand level with Mary's head. We hit the dirt tumbling as his men raised their guns. I caught a sidelong glance of Mary pulling the two girls, gagged and bound, behind the fence and out of sight—not sure what had happened to the giant in the black suit. I had to assume the girls would be safe with her. I was in enough trouble of my own. A chorus of clicks and clacks filled the air as a hundred weapons were racked and readied. I rolled up off Joey and took a boxing stance as he came up dusting the desert sand from his Armani.

"Not really suitable attire, Joe," I taunted. "Sorry about your car, by the way. I think I might have scratched the paint."

"Yeah, we found it back there in the desert, you fuck!" He spat at my feet as he shrugged off his jacket and tossed it on top of the nearest car. "Where's the record, motherfucker?"

"Up your ass."

"Fuck you, Irish faggot."

"Nice talk. How's your ass feeling these days, Joey? I heard some friends of mine made a woman out of you."

I hated having to resort to his level, but it might distract him long enough for the girls to get to safety.

He was a maniac, and like all maniacs, nothing could hold his attention more than defending his own lunacy. He took a wide swing at me and missed.

I knew his type: real tough when he had six or seven guys behind him, not so impressive when the fight was fair.

"Not much of a boxer, are you, Nancy?" I laughed and popped him a jab in the chin. I wasn't even trying to hurt him, just goad him into a fight to distract him from having his goombahs open fire and start a bloodbath. "I hear you suck a mean dick, though!" I swatted him with a left hook in the jaw.

"*Fuck you!*" he screamed, and lunged at me.

I easily sidestepped him and clapped him with a cross to the back of his ear.

Now he was getting angry. Little men like Joey, used to bullying and hurting people by proxy, or when they're tied up and defenceless, always got upset when you toyed with them and made them look weak. They tended to get especially perturbed when you questioned their sexuality. Faux manliness breeded some seriously high-octane homophobia.

I hated that shit, but I had to keep him occupied.

"Come on, Joey," I teased. "I thought you were *hard*. Or is that just when you've got another guy's balls in your mouth?"

He went apeshit and started flailing his arms before he shot forward and tackled me into the dust. I used the momentum to flip mid-air and land on top, pinning Joey to the ground with my legs. His men were still standing frozen, staring down the barrels of a hundred Mexican guns. They were paying little to no attention to their boss and his schoolyard hissy fit.

"*Get the fuck offa me, you cunt!*" He struggled underneath me.

"That's not nice, Joey. Play nice." I slapped him in the face, and gave him the paintbrush, back and forth across the face until his cheeks were purple. "Call off your fucking goons and maybe I'll let you up." Schoolyard justice.

"*Kiss my ass!*"

He managed to get one arm loose and I found myself lost in a haze of dust as he hurled a handful of sand up into my face. I jumped back by reflex, and was clawing the stinging cloud away from my eyes, when a burning pain shot through my thigh. I collapsed under my own weight and watched Joey scramble away, then noticed the handle of his knife jutting out of my leg. My jeans were turning dark in a quickly spreading stain as the blood poured down into my shoes. I fought to keep my head from spinning as I realized that the blade was surely buried nearly straight through the bone.

"*Shoot this motherfucker!*" Joey was screaming at no one in particular.

"Um, boss, I don't think that's a good idea," one of them responded.

I couldn't tell where the voice came from. It was all I could do to keep my eyeballs from rolling back into my brain. I lay back in the dirt, trying desperately to avoid the instinct to yank the knife out, knowing that I'd certainly bleed to death, or at least bleed out faster.

Joey's men slowly backed up towards the cars as Joey jumped and stomped and hollered and demanded that they shoot me.

"Boss, I think we should get out of here."

"*Nobody is paying you to think! Shoot this motherfucker!*"

Poor Joey, nobody was listening to him. He had an absolute fit, stomping and screaming and throwing his hands up in the air.

I couldn't hear what he was saying—maybe I was dying—but a tremendous roar filled the air and wind swirled around me like a tornado.

Joey Thumbs stopped dead in his tracks and looked up to the sky. Now he was yelling at the sky, shaking his fist. The roar became deafening and Joey's men ducked into the cars. Now it was like the flapping of huge wings, *thump-thump-thump-thump.*

I tried to sit up but the force of air coming down pushed me back down. It was helicopters—two big ugly helicopters. More Oliver Stone bullshit. Joey was hiding behind one of the cars, and I could see his fucking alligator shoes under the car.

All of a sudden, someone was pulling on me. Strong arms dragged me back through the sand. My leg bounced over rocks and sent screaming lightning bolts of pain through my body and into my brain. Each one shuddered up my spine like a cold snap before exploding into white light behind my eyes.

I was dropped somewhere behind the fence, and looked up into the face of an angel.

"Are you okay, Musclemoe?"

A surge of energy shot through me and I sat bolt upright, throwing my arms around her and squeezing the little girl so tight, I thought I'd break her. I laughed as tears streamed down my face. My body was on fire, but I hadn't been happier in my entire life.

"Oh, baby-girl, I am fantastic!" I released my bear hug on her and held her face in my hands.

"Are you okay? They didn't hurt you? You're all right?" I asked while frantically scanning her for injuries.

She smiled at me with that sweet, innocent smile. "I'm okay. You didn't come to see Lego Land, Monsemmo."

"No, I didn't get a chance yet, Sweetheart. I will. I promise I will. Where's your Mom?"

"She's over there." She pointed towards the fence where Rosie stood, next to her Grandmother. "You got a knife in your leg," she added innocently. Then, with determined anger, Holly said, "That jerk hit my Mom. I hope you kicked his butt!"

"I got my licks in, kid." I chuckled and dusted her hair.

Jorge appeared from out of nowhere with a man he said was a doctor. "He will remove the knife, Cole. You must be brave now, this will hurt."

I made Holly go with Jorge to hide inside the house, and bit down on my own arm as the doctor first wiggled, then worked the knife loose, then yanked it from my leg with a geyser of red and a muffled scream. Another man ran over with something hot, and the heat passed my face as he waved it towards the doctor.

I knew what was coming, but had little time to prepare for it before nearly dropping from the searing agony of muscles and skin cooking. I got a nose full of pan-seared Cole, and screamed out in more pain than I'd ever felt in my interminable existence. And I've been shot—on multiple occasions.

Suddenly Rosie was at my side, holding my weak hand in hers and running her fingers through my hair.

The doctor said something in Spanish.

"*¿qué?*" I muttered.

"*La pierna será buena otra vez. Curará. Curará. ¿usted entiende? Curará.*" He stumbled back toward the house.

"What did he say?" Rosie asked as she gingerly wrapped a bandage around my leg.

"He said it'll be fine. Joey Thumbs, did he hurt you?"

"Nothing I couldn't handle."

I sat up and looked at her face, all purple on one side, with a lip swollen and split.

"I'll fucking kill him," I said, touching the bruise gently with my fingertips.

"Who is she?" Rosie asked, looking off towards Mary.

"That," I replied, "is Mary Ramirez, formerly Stetch. She's your grandmother." No sense in pulling punches at a party like this.

Rosie gasped, then caught herself and, much as her grandmother would have, straightened her back and recalled her composure, resetting herself by the reality she clung to.

"That's impossible. My grandmother died. Dad said...." She looked at me with those deep, magnificent emerald eyes, pleading with me not to let her whole world fall apart.

I felt terrible, mostly for the things she'd endured because of me, but she deserved to know the truth. She deserved to have a better family than the old prick who'd been lying to her since the day she was born.

"Dad lied. About everything," I assured her, immediately dropping my head in shame. I couldn't bear to see her heart broken one more time, not from something I'd said.

Rosie looked off after her grandmother again and sighed in resignation. She knew what her father was, and she knew he'd never uttered a single honest word to her in her life. I hauled myself up to my feet, balancing myself on her shoulder, and she took me in with a look of battered confusion that quickly turned to concern.

"Where the hell do you think you're going?" she demanded.

"He said it would be all right. Besides, this isn't anywhere near over yet. I assume that was either the D.E.A. or a small army of Japanese businessmen?"

"They might have been Japanese," she said, surprised. "They have your friend with them."

"What? Who?"

"The rock star."

"Aw, fuck me," I said, hobbling off towards the gates. "*Danny?*" I hollered.

My old friend Mr. Ken Nakadaka of the Oyabun Corporation stood at the fence, awaiting my shambling approach. I peered behind him to see the company logo on the sides of the helicopters, and Danny waving wildly from the open door of one of the birds.

"We have brought your friend, the drunken baboon, as collateral, Mr. Cole." Nakadaka stepped towards the fence.

"I think you mean *buffoon.*"

"No, he said he prefers baboon."

"Yeah, okay, I can see that."

"Mr. Fox was quite insistent that you may be having trouble with some gentlemen from Las Vegas that you could use our assistance with."

I bowed to Nakadaka in deference to his less-than-charitable assist. "You have already proven that assistance, Nakadaka. Thank you. But I don't have the record here."

"Please don't underestimate us, Mr. Cole. We know you have it, and we would like to complete our transaction. We have one million dollars, in cash, and your friend. You have the record."

"Well, it's not quite so simple, Kenny."

"You are not as amusing as you imagine yourself to be, Mr. Cole. I would suggest we complete our transaction and get on with our separate existence as soon as possible. That is, if you wish to remain in the good graces of my employers."

I was about to add another witty retort to the exchange when we were interrupted by a scream. It was the scream of a little girl.

I turned and ran, more out of blind panic than decision, and hit the corner running, or as close to it as I could manage with a gaping hole in my thigh, and fell into the door of the main house just as Rosie and Mary were running out hollering for me. My leg gave out and I stumbled.

Mary grabbed my arm and pulled me back to standing with a fierce strength that demonstrated her own level of anxiety. "*He's got Holly!*" she screamed in my face.

"Who? Who has Holly?"

"That gangster! That fucking gangster has my baby!" She wrestled out of my arms and screamed into the dry air, "*I'll fucking kill you!*"

"Rosie. *Rosie!*" I shook her roughly by the shoulders to snap her out of her Mama Bear fury. "Where did he take her?"

"*Fucking kill you!*" she bellowed.

Mary interrupted. "Cole, he took her out through the back. The only place he could hide back there is in the fields."

I stood frozen for a moment, Rosie twisting in my grip, my leg a blazing inferno of pain. The solution came to me in a flash, and I let go of Rosie, who crumpled to the ground in a wail of misery, Mary rushing to console her.

I bolted, dragging my leg behind me, back to the fence and the Yakuza general. "Nakadaka, I need your helicopter. Right now."

Chapter 26

Moments later, the bird was back in the sky, turning tight circles around the seemingly endless fields of pot plants growing seven feet high. It was like one more scene out of that damn Kubrick flick.

I worked my way into the fields through wall after wall of tall stalks, and the unmistakable tangy odor of reefer, as Nakadaka and ten of Mary Ramirez's men relayed their positions through headset walkie-talkies, all of us trying hard to be nothing more than whispers in the grass. The helicopter roared over us and shortly flattened the plants, as Danny bellowed through his headset that they hadn't found him yet.

I would occasionally stop and call out to Holly, reassuring her everything would be all right, and then reminding Joey Thumbs that he was all alone with nowhere to go and half a dozen men with guns looking for him. It took about ten minutes before I got a reply.

"Fuck you, Cole. You come any closer and some pothead in Malibu will be smoking this little girls brains."

"Joey, think about this. What's gonna happen, huh? You hurt the girl, we're still gonna get you, but then you'll be facing an angry mob as a child-killer, instead of a *man of respect*. What would DeFrancesco say about this, Joe?"

I hunted quietly through the weeds, trying not to give myself away, but trying to cover enough ground to find Joey and give the others time to home in on the tracking signal from my headset. Whatever else I might say about the Yakuza, they definitely got the best toys.

"Just let the girl go, Joey," I called out. "She doesn't need to be a part of this."

"You know what didn't need to be a part of this, Cole? You frying my nuts like a couple of oysters, motherfucker. I'm gonna take this little cupcake out of here and have her kiss my balls better. What do you think, Cole? You think she'd make a nice little *bocchinara*? I bet I could get her to work it pretty good. Oh yeah! She'd make a nice little whore for me and my boys."

His voice seemed to be coming from all directions. I couldn't pin down where he was, and between the blood loss from my leg and the blood pounding in my head from rage, listening to this maniac talk about hurting innocent little Holly, I was hopelessly lost in the wilderness.

"Why don't you come out here and face me like a man, you piece of shit!"

"Why don't you roast, motherfucker!"

He was behind me.

I whirled to face him and was hit in the face with a billowing cloud of acrid smoke. I twisted too fast and my leg gave out beneath me, and I fell crashing to my knees, enveloped in the fumes.

Thumbs' voice echoed behind the curtain of smoke. "I told you... you're gonna get yours, dick. Reap the fuckin' whirlwind."

"*Let her go, Thumbs!*" I coughed, trying to mask the pain and weakness that were currently preventing me from standing, let alone escaping the maelstrom that was building around me.

"I'm gonna fuck you dead, Cole. Then I'm gonna turn this little girl out for tricks." He laughed, hearty and uproarious, all around me.

My head was swimming in it. I couldn't escape. Stars flashed in my sight and the edges of my vision began to fade out. I was falling away from myself, sputtering on smoke and twisting in the wind. The smoke made my lungs ache and my head feel like a helium balloon. I was pretty sure I could just lie down and go to sleep. Wouldn't that be fuckin' nice, I told myself. *Yessiree Bob.*

My rational mind fought to maintain some kind of control over my weakening body and my pot-addled brain. I was going to die just like Joey Thumbs wanted, roasted alive and okay with it. Then, just as I was about to lie back and welcome the Fire Gods, one word snapped me out of it completely, and brought me to my feet like a thundering gladiator with one last chance for glory.

"Mossimo!" It was Holly. "Mossimo! Help!"

I was already gauging where they were behind the thick wall of grey fog when I heard the slap and heard her little voice cry out in pain.

"Shut up, you little bitch!"

I was going to kill that sonofabitch if it required the last breath in my body. Before I could relay that message, another cry rang out, this time from Thumbs.

"Ow! You little cunt! You burn with him then!"

Holly cried out again, but this time her voice was moving closer towards me, coughing and crying.

I dove forward into the smoke to find her, and waved frantically through the fumes trying to reach her, trying to force the image of a little girl engulfed in flames out of my mind.

"Holly? *Holly!* Follow my voice, Sweetie."

"I've got ye, brother," came through the headset as the smoke momentarily parted under the pounding wind of the helicopter.

Holly stumbled through the flaming shoots of marijuana, slapping at the arms of her dress and stumbling forward through the fire. She coughed and weaved, as if she were moving in slow motion.

Things were still moving that slowly when the arm come through behind her, gun levelled towards her.

I ran as hard as a leg and a half could carry me, shouting for her to drop to the ground. She turned and dove to one side just as she cleared the smouldering bushes, and Joey Thumbs emerged like a ghost through whispering tendrils of smoke.

I stopped dead in my tracks, trying to turn the pivot and dive in the opposite direction, but I wasn't getting anywhere on my damaged stump of a leg. I heard the first three cracks of the gun, rapid-fire, and felt the pressure of the air slamming into my head, one side and then the other. Then hot metal tore through me, throwing me back into the plants behind, leaving no breath in me at all.

I was shot, probably dying. Hell, I was lucky to be alive even before I took the bullet. But my first thought was Holly.

I rolled, sucking hard to get a good breath, but all I managed was flames in my chest, and enough of a view to see Holly standing, crying and screaming out my name, as Joey Thumbs stepped towards me with his gun at his side and an evil grin tearing his face open like a goblin. My ears had stopped working, and everything was a blur of silent imagery. I blinked and turned my eyes from my encroaching doom, to the sweet little girl who was about to watch me die.

So this is how it ends, not with a bang, or a whimper... just inevitability ringing in your ears.

Then came the miracle.

People always talk about miracles as if they're some kind of Divine intervention, God Himself reaching out and changing the game in your favor, dropping an ace where you only had a four of clubs. The truth was that a miracle happened when you absolutely gave up hope, and then some crazy drunken Irishman swooped down from a helicopter and snatched up a little girl from the middle of a burning slaughterhouse.

I almost didn't register what I'd seen, and would have thought it was a fever dream, or a final death knell hallucination from the exorbitant amount of THC I'd been inhaling, but Joey Thumbs stopped cold and stood looking at the sky, dumfounded, just long enough for me to understand the reality of the situation.

The chopper came out of the smoke, goddamn *Apocalypse Now*, swooping in with Danny hanging from a rope ladder. He flew in like a superhero, grabbing Holly with one arm as he clung to the ladder with the other, then they disappeared again into the hazy hereafter.

When the surreal moment of abject wonder had passed, I summoned my last ten ounces of strength and rolled to reach the .45 tucked in my waistband. I flung blindly toward my nemesis and pulled the trigger, and the explosion shot up my arm. I bucked back and lost hold of the grip, the pistol flying off to be lost in the brush.

Joey Thumbs stood unharmed, still bewildered, and patted himself down for bullet holes. When he was satisfied that he was unscathed, he marched toward me like an angry father with a belt, ready to show me the error of my ways.

He was saying something, but I couldn't hear a damn thing, just a constant tide rolling in my head, barely muting the air raid sirens in my ears. I tried to gather what he was shouting by the movement of his lips, but I was no lip reader.

"I can't hear you, fuckface!" I yelled back at him.

I *think* I yelled it. It was a muffled moan inside my own head, so who knows what he heard. I was using what little precious life I had left to find that goddamn pistol. If I was going, I was damn sure taking him with me. Unfortunately, I was down to one good hand, and with my smoke-irritated eyes pouring like waterfalls, I couldn't have found a blue whale if I'd been sitting on top of it. I managed to make out scuffed and weed-encrusted Gucci loafers, as Thumbs stepped over me before he nudged me over with his foot, so that I was staring straight up into the barrel of his gun. I closed my eyes and waited for the end.

I knew it was the end because Frank was playing inside my head. I could still hear that.

"THERE WERE TIMES,

"I'M SURE YOU KNEW....

"I BIT OFF....

"MORE THAN I COULD CHEW...."

And now the end is near, Frankie. The end seemed to have something to do with a 170-lb sack of shit falling on me and crushing out the last of my breath. As the world went black, the last of my senses leaving me, a warm flood of something soaked my chest.

"I ATE IT UP AND SPIT IT OUT....

"I FACED IT ALL....

"I STOOD TALL....

"I DID IT...."

Chapter 27

I woke to the sound of giggling, and opened my eyes to dim light, surrounded by white — white ceiling, to be exact. White ceiling and a *beep... beep... beep...* and then giggling and soft moans.

"Oh, Mr. Thunders... we really shouldn't...."

I was waking up in my worst nightmare: I'd been resurrected as one of Danny's road-trip roommates.

"Don't worry, Sweetness. Nobody'll hear, and he's out cold."

I turned my head, slowly, and realized where I was — the beeping, the white ceiling and walls, Danny nailing a nurse behind that curtain on the next bed over.

"What the hell?" It came out as more of a groan than actual words. I cleared my very dry throat and felt the pressure of a tube running down my nostril into who knows where. I tried again.

"The hell is going on here?" I managed. It sounded something like Abe Vigoda belching into a fan.

"Did you hear something?" came the woman's voice.

"No, love, just the pounding of me heart and the commingling of our loins."

"Danny?" I croaked.

"Sweet fuckin' hell!" Danny came tumbling out from under the curtain in a heap, jumping to his feet while simultaneously yanking his tightie-whities and his jeans up at the same time. It was something he had a lot of practice with.

"*Mossy boy!*" he hollered, dancing like an excited puppy.

I could smell the whiskey radiating from him, but I didn't care. I was glad to see his face.

"Holly? Rosie? Okay?" It rumbled slowly from the back of my throat like a scratchy old record on the wrong speed.

"Yer young ladies are well." He smiled, but weakly, as if waiting for me to kick the bucket right there.

"What happened?" I grumbled, as the admittedly pretty nurse scrambled to put herself together while checking the machines next to my head.

She smelled like vanilla and honey and had a tiny, star-shaped tattoo on her hip. Danny gave her a wink and a pinch on the thigh before he turned back to answer my question.

"Ye been shot, Mossy!" He settled into a chair next to me, regaining his old self with a look of relief I'd never imagined seeing on that face. "That Thumbs fella put a couple o' bullets in ye, which, on top o' being stabbed through the leg and having the shit kicked out of ye repeatedly, seemed to leave ye worse for wear. He laid a couple past yer head as well, nearly blew yer fuckin' ears off. Luckily for me, ye should be fine to slap the ol' bass in no time."

The nurse turned to leave, still zipping her uniform, but Danny jumped from his chair, caught her by one arm and spun her into his chest, laying what looked like a very intimate goodbye on her before ushering her on her way by grabbing a handful of her left ass cheek.

"Next time, love. Call me!" He turned back to me. "God I love a woman in a fuckin' uniform!"

I thought of trying to rein him in with a holler, or a smack, as I would normally have done, but I seriously lacked energy for much more than breathing and keeping my eyes open.

"Fortunately for ye, fella," he continued, "ye had ingested so much of that reefer smoke that they barely had to sedate ye to get those bullets out and fix yer sorry ass up. 'Course, ye've been unconscious for eight days, but what's one week baked in a coma? A stitch in time, eh?"

"A week?" I whispered. "Mob. DeFrancesco. Girls safe...."

"Not to worry, lad." He smiled. "That Mary Rodriguez took care of it all. She is some kind of woman. If I was a hundred years old, I'd be climbin' her like an oak tree. She sorted it."

"What? Sorted how?" I mumbled.

"Well, she made a deal with our dear Nakadaka, gave him the record for his boss in exchange for the million and flying yer sorry ass in to the hospital. He was none too happy to have ye bleedin' all over his pretty helicopter, I don't mind tellin'."

"But DeFrancesco?"

"We took care of it. Paid a visit to the Swede. He knew a guy who knew a guy.... They rigged up a ringer. Perfect copy. Aged it and everythin'. Couldn't tell the difference if you tried. Y'know, that foulmouthed little bastard is all right, although now I have to take the whole band in for a free gig. They're not gonna like that.'

I tried to laugh and found the result something like coughing spaghetti out your nose while having a heart attack. "Joey Thumbs?"

"Right-O. Guess ye weren't really paying attention at the time."

He winked and came in close to give me his secret. "After I plucked the young lady from the very arms of death, we swung back around and found Thumbs laying all over ye." He cocked his fingers at my head like a gun, something that had taken on newfound significance.

"I don't... shot me... he...."

"He was dead as bloody Dillinger. I think they buried him out there in their marijuana field. Guess ye got lucky with that last bullet, boyo."

"Last?"

"Ye were lying under him, all shot to shit, with an empty pistol in yer hand."

Lucky doesn't begin to describe it. The last thing I remember, I was still fumbling through the dirt looking for it and Thumbs had me dead to rights.

"DeFrancesco?"

"Mary again. She herself went to the lair of the white worm and gave him the dupe record. Charmed him with some stories and they worked out some kind of deal. I'd imagine the other fellas who ran out on Thumbsie that day, and the fact that he kidnapped a little girl, probably helped paint the picture of a maniac on the loose, and that ain't good business no matter which mob ye run with.'

I heaved as deep a breath as my lousy body would allow, and felt a swell of relief wash over me.

"You saved her. Saved Holly."

He gave me his standard sly smile and waved me off, but I knew him better than any other person on Earth, and I could see tears threatening to corrupt his devilish eyes. I was honestly surprised that he didn't start right off bragging about it, but I guess even a life-long swaggering braggart like Foxy Thunders could have a change of ways.

"Nothin' to it. I wasn't about to let that sweet little girl see ye take it like Sonny Corleone."

I smiled and squeezed his hand.

A mist rose in his eyes, but he immediately shook it off and smirked. "'Sides, another ten years and I'll be looking to sneak her friends in backstage. Always helps to have an in with the ladies." He laughed.

Cocky bastard. Cocky, disgusting bastard.

The doctors came rushing in, yammering about bullet trajectories, narrowly missed arteries, one-in-a-million chances... *blah blah blah.* Long story short? I was lucky to be alive, luckier still to be in close to one piece. They explained that I'd be stuck there for another week or so, at which point they'd take out tubes and probes, and I could eat, drink, take a piss. I nodded my head, thanked them for saving me, and promised to be good.

Danny excused himself politely, something I never imagined I'd see in my lifetime. He slapped my face and kissed my cheek, and then I was surrounded by white jackets and clipboards. I caught him glancing back with what I thought looked like concern, but my eyes suddenly got very heavy.

I decided to let sleep take me properly, for once.

***

When I woke again, it was to a dark and empty room, the steady beeping and ticking of the machines hovering around me like some technological entourage. I managed, with some small grief and a lot of effort, to sit up and reach for the call button. I was parched. I couldn't remember ever having been so goddamn thirsty before in my life. What I saw lying on the table next to the bed made me forget all about my dry throat and cotton-mouth.

It was my name—my name in her slow, looping cursive. An envelope for me.

I scrambled to clutch it and hold it in my hands, to catch even the faintest whiff of her, just to know she'd really been here, that she really existed at all. I reached out for it and found myself tangled and pulled and held back by wires and tubes. I tugged once with half-hearted hope, slipping my feet to the floor and weakly leaning forward, then lost my shit altogether. I wrapped my arm through them like Hercules about to move a mountain, and tore the works from the machines—and my arms—and hot blood spurted up my forearms.

A howling pain resonated through my shoulder and chest, but I was free. I had the envelope in my hands before I heard him rustling behind me.

"Jesus, Cole."

"How long you been sitting here in the dark, Danny?"

"All fuckin' night, lad."

My heart sank as I realized why.

"I don't want to read this, do I?"

"I don't reckon ye have a choice, boyo."

It wasn't sealed. I slipped out the letter and a slim piece of paper—a check—and felt the complete absence of all the passion and life that had just been coursing through me moments before. I sank to the bed as the nurses rushed in hollering, thinking me a goner when my machines all went dead. I was wishing they'd been right.

They surrounded me like white-garbed angels, lifting me back into the bed and administering their needles and probes. When they were finished, I turned my head to look at Danny, hoping there weren't tears in my eyes, though I knew there were.

"A check?" I croaked at him, voice cracking in a million places simultaneous to my heart. "A fucking check? What does the letter say?"

Danny looked as if his own heart was breaking, one of the hundred reasons I knew he'd always be there for me, even as the women came and went.

He pulled a new flask from inside of his jacket and took a long pull. "I don't know, Moss."

"What did she *say*?" I demanded.

"I don't know." He lowered his eyes. "Yer gonna have to read it for yerself, lad."

I pushed the heels of my hands into my eyes, hoping to both stem the flow of certain tears and push the fear and loathing and misery out of my head. All I really accomplished was to make myself see a cascade of black spots as I unfolded the letter and forced myself to read.

When I'd read it, re-read it, and considered tearing, crumpling, and burning it in effigy, I turned back to Danny. This time the tears welled up, but I didn't give a shit anymore. I 'd been beaten, stabbed, shot, torn apart, and then run through a trash compactor. None of that compared to the pain that she had inflicted.

I looked at my friend and could tell that he knew the score. "Why didn't you tell me this afternoon?"

"You just came out of a goddamned coma, Cole. I wasn't about to tell ye that yer redheaded goddess was running out on ye. I know ye better than anyone ever has, better than Moe Rossi himself. I know ye were putting all yer eggs in that basket—wife, kid, instant life. Problem is, both of ye are fucked as the day is long. She's running away from her shitty family, and ye've always been chasing the one ye lost. I'm sorry, brother. Really, truly sorry."

I lay back and reflected on that last part. He was right, of course. Mouthy little fucker was always right. I had been chasing something, chasing it hard.

I tossed the letter aside and stared at the check. "This money is from Mary Stetch."

"She thought ye deserved a bonus. Ye did just more or less broker her a million-dollar deal."

"This is half of it."

"She's got money. So does Rose, and little Holly. They're gonna be fine."

"I'm not going to be fine, Danny. She was the one."

"And how, exactly, do you figure that? After four days? Come on, Moss."

"I should have died in that field."

"And you didn't."

"I wish I had."

Danny's hand came out of nowhere, and my teeth rattled in the back of my skull.

"*Enough!*" He pulled his chair up and put his face in mine, eyes blazing with that hot Irish temper.

"I am sick to fuckin' hell of listening to ye whine and mope. Everything comes so fuckin' easy to ye. Ye speak twelve languages, and play thirty instruments. Ye lost yer virginity to fuckin' royalty! Ye get more arse than Tom fuckin' Jones!"

"You're the one banging nurses in my hospital room."

"Fuck you. I get women because I'm famous. Ye get em' because yer the fuckin' *man*. Ye don't even know it, do ye? Always down on yerself. Lost yer family, poor little Mossy. Lost yer grandpa, so ye have to be just like him, poor fragile little boy. Fuck you, man. Fuck. You."

"Danny—"

"Ye had Eva fucking *Priest* take you into her bed. The Lonely Madame herself."

"Danny—"

"That there is a lot of fuckin' zeroes, Mossimo Cole. Retire from this Shamus bullshit and go see the world. Come play with me! Action! Adventure! New sexy lady in every port! Like fuckin' pirates, Moss!" He was up and dancing around now, anger spent, back to his snappy, carefree self. "Now, then, ye need a drink?" He held the flask out to me with a wink.

"Maybe you can go grab me some water? Or a coffee. I'd kill for some goddamn coffee."

He smirked, took another swig, and launched himself from the chair to lay a big kiss on the side of my face, then paused as he stood to leave.

He reached in his pocket and set a tiny pile of plastic on my chest.

"Little Miss Holly made me promise to give that to ye." He turned away with a hitch in his voice.

It was a flower. A Lego flower.

Chapter 28

They'd said it would take me six weeks to leave the hospital.
 I was out in three.

***

I staked out her apartment for days, and talked to Stetch. He was a broken old man, more confused than ever. He didn't remember the record, and barely remembered Rosie. Eventually, I pieced together that she had seen him a few days after the gunfight at the ganja corral. He didn't know anything else. If she told him where she was going, it didn't stick. He just lay there, hands still bandaged, face still bruised, a ghost of the miserable prick he once was.

Mary Ramirez refused my calls, so I had Danny drive me back to Gomez Palacio. He bitched and complained and joked all the way, trying to talk me out of it, trying to convince me to go back to Never-Never Land and be one of the wild boys.

It took me five minutes to convince Jorge to let me speak to his mother. It took me the rest of the day to convince her to listen. She looked like she was going to have me made into a purse when I reached for the trumpet on the wall of her study, but when I forced my weak, crippled body to fill with air and send a song across the ages for her, she wept.

I let the strains of *Stormy Weather* take her back to 1948, before she knew misery and terror and pain. I put every ounce of my soul and my life into that song, praying it would move her enough to give me the one chance I so desperately needed.

When I finished, she wiped the tears from her eyes and wrapped her arms around me like the grandmother I never knew. Jorge took me into another parlour and plied me with a rich Mexican coffee, while Danny sat fidgeting and flipping through Spanish novels he couldn't read.

When she returned, it was with the horn in one hand, and a scrap of paper in the other. "Meet her here, day after tomorrow, noon sharp."

I looked at the paper: *Lego Land. North Entrance. Noon.*

"Thank you, Mary," I said, tears welling in my eyes. "Thank you."

"Don't thank me yet, Cole. She is a stubborn woman and she has her reasons for leaving you behind. I hope she'll listen to your reasons for making her stay. You're a good man."

She held the trumpet out to me, taking my hand and placing it on the valves, gently. I looked at her with questioning eyes.

"I want you to have it. He would have wanted that," she explained, eyes still wet with tears.

"Mary, I can't—"

"Thank you," she insisted, "for bringing our daughter back to us, in a very special way. Now I feel like Georgie can finally rest in peace."

Danny snuck a few bottles of tequila and a sizable bag of green from our guests, and we drove away to little fanfare. Mary Ramirez and her son stood at the gates of Estado del Ramirez, waving like family as we barreled off into the afternoon sun.

Danny didn't speak until we were halfway to Hermosillo. I'd been dozing off in the passenger seat, still feeling weak and sickly, clutching the trumpet like a teddy bear. The sound of his voice startled me out of near-slumber.

"What are ye going to do if she says no?"

I looked at his face, eerily lit by the dashboard lights. Danny was my family. He really was my brother, and the only one who'd stayed with me through this whole shitty ordeal.

I'd had plenty of visitors—Charlie Moses, Kickerdick and Manlove, and Mrs. Bradley, who brought me homemade soup that smelled like hot garbage mixed with lead paint. Even Lacy Lincoln had come by to pay her respects, in skin-tight pants and an open-necked shirt that gave me a full view of the goods when she leaned over the bed and licked at what was left of my earlobe. All of them were transient beings, in and out of my periphery, just like they were in and out of my life.

Danny had cancelled five shows and a recording session to stay at my side. He'd brought me coffee and music and sat in the room, just to be there for me. He'd paid my bills and checked my mail, and talked to my doctors. He'd led me on walks and refused to listen to my whining and my heartbreak, and had taken me to Stetch and even driven me to another country.

"Danny, why the hell have you put up with me this long?" I asked him from underneath my coat.

"Ye remember when we first met? We were, what? Twelve? Ye and Pops came to stay at Ma's."

"Yeah, we were only supposed to stay for a couple of days, and we ended up staying for two months because Pops said he liked your Ma's cooking so much. I think it was really because I'd found a friend."

Danny pulled a left-handed cigarette out of his shirt pocket and let the window down before he lit it, sucking deep and holding in a breath before he continued. "Pops had been coming there for years before. I think he and Ma had a thing goin'. Y'know how he loved the redheads."

"Your Ma was pretty hot back then—"

"The fuck? I'm tellin' a story here, boyo. Anyways, me Da' was a right miserable drunken bastard, if ye'll recall. If he even *was* me Da'…"

I vaguely remembered Danny's dad as a crumbling drunk who would disappear for days at a time, and once laid a beating on twelve-year-old Danny for spilling a pint. I found out later that Danny had taken a beating like that four times a week from his old man. Pops didn't intervene, which I never understood, but Danny's father vanished for good not long after, which I'd always wondered about.

"Da' gave me that last beatin' and Moe Rossi took him out back. Ma told me that Da' had to go to hospital. He never did come back, not that we weren't better off. I never told ye, but when Ma died, she told me that yer Pops told him that if he ever laid a hand on me again, that he'd kill him, and he took it serious enough to never return. I loved yer Pops, same as ye. He was a good man, Moss. So are ye—just as good. Better even. Ye just don't see it because yer so busy always trying to prove yerself to a ghost. Ye need to let go. Ye need to move on."

I let it stand and didn't say anything else for a long time. We drove in silence to the border, where we switched seats. I promised I was well enough to drive for a while and let him sleep. When we crossed paths at the back of the car, I grabbed him and held on for dear life, in spite of the pain raging in every part of my upper body.

"Thank you, Danny. I love you."

"Ye poncey twat." He smiled. "Let's get to Lego Land already."

***

Danny dropped me off in front at 11:50 and, with ticket in hand, I stood shivering despite the heat, my skin crawling with nervous energy. I eyeballed every figure that moved in my periphery, whipped my head toward every sound, until I saw her standing in front of the gift shop.

She stood still and quiet, waiting for me to approach. Her face was more tanned than I remembered, but her lips were just as full and red. Her eyes spoke piteous volumes, pleading with me to leave. I could see my own heartbreak reflected in those emerald eyes, even from ten feet away.

"Hi," she finally offered. "I'm glad you're okay."

"Yep. Right as rain," I replied from some hollow place inside me. It echoed in my head.

"I'm sorry, Moss."

"I know." It was as bold a lie as I've ever told, but seemed like the way these things were supposed to play out.

"I've been looking for you for weeks," I said. "Why didn't you come to the hospital? What did I do?"

"You saved us. You changed us. I don't know, Moss. It's... different now."

I bridged the gap between us and took her hands in mine, staring down into her face, daring her eyes to meet mine and stay there.

"Exactly. Different. Good different, right?"

"Just different. Look, it was fun, and I really like you, but...."

I panicked and backed away, hands moving to my face in exasperation. "But what, Rosie? I'm not good enough for you now? I'm not rich enough?" It was a low blow, and even I knew it was patently untrue, but I was hurt, backed into a corner, feeling the pull of the downward spiral this conversation was destined to take.

"You're just too... much. Too dangerous, too wild, too unpredictable. I have just had my whole life flipped over. I need time to sort it out and I think you're too dangerous for Holly to be around. In less than a week she was almost killed twice! I know it wasn't exactly your fault, but...."

"Rosie, please."

"Goodbye, Cole," she said, smiling weakly as she turned to walk away. "I'm sorry. Good luck."

"Yeah. Say goodbye to Holly for me. Tell her I'll miss her."

I felt empty and used-up, like a beer glass with the blood, spit and cigarette butts from the previous night's violence all sitting in the bottom of me.

I hung my head, stuffed my hands in my pockets, and turned to walk away. Out of the corner of my eye I saw her, watching, tucked into a shadow by the door.

I was almost to the exit turnstile when she hit my legs and I felt my knees buckle, just barely keeping my balance as she wrapped herself around my calf.

"Don't go!" she cried. "You promised to come to Lego land with me!"

"And I came, Sweetheart," I said, sinking painfully down to one knee and pulling her away from me.

Those big eyes looked up at me, full of hurt, tiny tears running down her face.

"Your mom doesn't think I should be around. She thinks I'm dangerous."

"You're not dangerous," she said, her little voice full of stubborn confidence. "That's stupid."

I laughed and pulled her back into my arms, hugging her for the last time, feeling my heart break one last, eternal time.

"Listen to your mom, Pumpkin. She's got your back. Here," I said, fishing a card from my pocket, "keep this. If you need me, or if your mom needs me, you know where to find me, okay?"

She gave me a quizzical look before staring down at the card for a moment.

"Oh!" she said, sounding genuinely surprised. "*Moss-i-mo!*"

She looked back up at me, then threw her arms around me as tightly as I believe any little girl could do.

"I love you, Mossimo. *Buona Notte.*"

I gently removed her arms, kissed her cheek, and stepped away. I had to. It was so goddamn hard, but I had to.

"*Buona Notte*, Angel. Take care of yourself, kid."

She blew me a kiss as I walked away, trying not to just break down and bawl like a baby in the middle of the parking lot. I looked back, just once, to see Rose standing with her, watching me leave, hugging her tight to her hip and wiping her eyes with her sleeve. Guess it wasn't just me—she must have felt it too, but it wasn't enough. It wasn't meant to be.

Danny was waiting, pained expression of understanding on his face. "Let's get ye a drink, fella." He fired up the engine.

Frank and Ella came on from the CD player: *Stormy Weather*. I rested my head back on the seat and let the joyful sorrow of their mingling voices wash over me like a velvet rain, and contemplated a nice, comforting glass of whiskey to drown my troubles.

Had it been worth it? All this trouble over a couple of songs?

I wouldn't have missed a minute of it.

"How about I buy *you* a cup of coffee, Danny boy?"

---Fini---

About the Author

Axel Howerton is most often described as: Badass Dad. Attendant Hubby. Author. Film/Music/Book reviewer. Time Lord. Bookhouse Boy. Coffee Addict. Dudeist. Sox National. Enmascarado. Reformed pugilist. Ink Monkey.

Axel is the long-time Managing Editor of *www.eyecrave.net*, and former Associate Editor of the horror fiction quarterly *Dark Moon Digest*. His work has appeared in *Kitschykoo Magazine, Beatroute, Dark Moon Digest, Dark Eclipse,* and *Big Pulp*, as well as on the websites *EWR: Short Stories, My Good Eye, The Den of Iniquity, ECDVD* and *Fires on the Plain* among many others. He has been included in the anthologies ***A Career Guide To Your Job In Hell***, ***Let It Snow*** and the upcoming book of essays ***Lebowski 101***. His work also appears in Arcana Comics *Steampunk Originals* #1 and the *Filthy Cake/Pit & Compendium* series. Axel's mini-collection ***Living Dead At Zigfreidt &*** Roy is available from most online retailers.

For more, please visit Axel Howerton online at:
Personal Website: http://axelhowerton.com/
Publisher Website: www.EvolvedPub.com
Goodreads: Axel_Howerton
Twitter: @AxelHow
Facebook: Thee.Axel.Howerton

Acknowledgements

With bottomless gratitude and all the love in my heart to my lovely wife and best friend, The Divine Ms. Liz; and to me boyos, Cole and Grady. Many thanks to the family who supported me and the friends who encouraged me—you know who you are and how much I owe. Much respect to all of the musicians, and music, referred to herein.

For their structural advice and architectural guidance, I tip my hat to the following: Shane MacDonald, Scott S. Phillips, Scott Duran, Mark Bonish, Amy Marshall, my ever-patient partner-in-crime Red Tash, and my beloved Ovalteens.

Molte grazie, tanto amore Dino Campitelli y Julie Jansen.

Many thanks to my editors, William Hampton and Lane Diamond, and to the entire Evolved Publishing team.

For Francis, and for Ryan Fox, both of whom left us far too soon. Here's to the heart, humanity, and raucous memories they left behind. Above all, this one is for my Grandad, MJH.

What's Next?

If you enjoyed *Hot Sinatra*, be sure to check out the origins of Manlove & Kickerdick in *Big Pulp's Summer 2013 LGBTQ* issue.

Axel Howerton is currently working on a steampunk novella for the *Empire of Steam & Rust* series to be released Spring 2013, and a YA sci-fi apocalypse comedy with his partner, Red Tash, also to be released sometime in 2013.

Several new novels and the further adventures of Moss Cole and his merry band of miscreants and oddballs are sure to follow.

Recommended Reading from Evolved Publishing:

CHILDREN'S PICTURE BOOKS
THE BIRD BRAIN BOOKS by Emlyn Chand:
> *Honey the Hero*
> *Davey the Detective*
> *Poppy the Proud*
> *Tommy Goes Trick-or-Treating*
> *Courtney Saves Christmas*
> *Vicky Finds a Valentine*

I'd Rather Be Riding My Bike by Eric Pinder
Valentina and the Haunted Mansion by Majanka Verstraete

HISTORICAL FICTION
Circles by Ruby Standing Deer
Spirals by Ruby Standing Deer
Stones by Ruby Standing Deer

LITERARY FICTION
Torn Together by Emlyn Chand
Hannah's Voice by Robb Grindstaff
Jellicle Girl by Stevie Mikayne
Weight of Earth by Stevie Mikayne

LOWER GRADE
THE THREE LOST KIDS – SPECIAL EDITION ILLUSTRATED
by Kimberly Kinrade:
> *Lexie World*
> *Bella World*
> *Maddie World*

THE THREE LOST KIDS – CHAPTER BOOKS by Kimberly Kinrade:
> *The Death of the Sugar Fairy*
> *The Christmas Curse*
> *Cupid's Capture*

MEMOIR
And Then It Rained: Lessons for Life by Megan Morrison

MYSTERY
Hot Sinatra by Axel Howerton

ROMANCE / EROTICA
Skinny-Dipping at Dawn by Darby Davenport
Walk Away with Me by Darby Davenport
Her Twisted Pleasures by Amelia James
His Twisted Lesson by Amelia James
Secret Storm by Amelia James
Tell Me You Want Me by Amelia James
The Devil Made Me Do It by Amelia James
Their Twisted Love by Amelia James

SCI-FI / FANTASY
Eulogy by D.T. Conklin

SHORT STORY ANTHOLOGIES
FROM THE EDITORS AT EVOLVED PUBLISHING:
    Evolution: Vol. 1 (A Short Story Collection)
    Evolution: Vol. 2 (A Short Story Collection)
    Pathways (A Young Adult Anthology)
All Tolkien No Action: Swords, Sorcery & Sci-Fi by Eric Pinder

SUSPENSE / THRILLER
Forgive Me, Alex by Lane Diamond
The Devil's Bane by Lane Diamond

YOUNG ADULT
Dead Embers by T.G. Ayer
Dead Radiance by T.G. Ayer
Farsighted by Emlyn Chand
Open Heart by Emlyn Chand
Pitch by Emlyn Chand
The Silver Sphere by Michael Dadich
Ring Binder by Ranee Dillon
Forbidden Mind by Kimberly Kinrade
Forbidden Fire by Kimberly Kinrade
Forbidden Life by Kimberly Kinrade
Forbidden Trilogy (Special Omnibus Edition) by Kimberly Kinrade
Desert Flower by Angela Scott
Desert Rice by Angela Scott
Survivor Roundup by Angela Scott
Wanted: Dead or Undead by Angela Scott

CPSIA information can be obtained at www.ICGtesting.com
Printed in the USA
LVOW07s1241050315

429274LV00012B/735/P